THIRTY SECONDS TO MIDNIGHT

CHRISTOPHER WILDE

ISBN: 978-1-3999-2001-8

1

The rain crashed down through the night, as I sat in my car on the edge of the cliff, waiting for the end of the world.

On the radio the ten o'clock news was long gone and had given way to a late-night DJ. He was sending the country to sleep with a series of ballads from the 1980s. I sat bolt-upright behind the wheel of the vehicle, every sinew in my body pulled tight. My leg bounced up and down in the footwell, but not to the beat of the music. The wait was excruciating.

I kept running through the plan in my head. It was absurd, but it might just work. And anyway, it was about as good an idea as I could come up with in just two days.

I held on to the slim chance that it might not be needed. That somehow, powerful people locked away in ostentatious rooms around the world, would see sense and prevent the inevitable. Was it really too late? Well if it wasn't, I reasoned that I hadn't burned any bridges; I could simply drive back down to London and head into work like any other day. Back to my normal job in IT security and my dull routine of commuting, work and microwaved meals. How I yearned for that banal routine now.

It was an eight hour drive from this remote Scottish coastline, but I'd be back in time for Monday morning. And besides, everyone had become so distracted the last couple of days that I doubted anyone would kick up a fuss if I missed a day or two.

If only. If only that would happen. But I knew it wouldn't. I wasn't exactly sure when the signal would come but it was bound to be soon. I'd expected it to have come by now and with each passing minute I'd grown hopeful. It was a reluctant hope, tinged with fear of the worst kind of disappointment, but I couldn't let it go.

My thoughts were interrupted when the radio cut out in the middle of a song and went silent. A short period of dead air gave way to a series of loud pips, the first of which made me jump. There was another silent break before a solemn voice cut in.

'This is BBC Scotland. Breaking news at this hour...'

It was happening.

2

'We are getting reports of a large explosion in London. These reports are coming in the main, from neighbouring counties, some several miles away. There have been numerous sightings of what is being described as a 'fire in the sky'. There is serious speculation that the explosion could have been caused by a...'

The newsreader's voice cracked. He coughed several times before continuing:

'Excuse me. There is serious speculation that the explosion could have been caused by a nuclear strike.'

It wasn't part of my plan to sit and listen to the whole story. I'd told myself that as soon as I heard a signal I'd get moving. But I was riveted to my seat. This was it. This was really, really, it. The beginning of the end.

Knowing something is going to happen and believing it will, are two entirely different things. Like a relative passing away after a long sickness, you know it's going to happen, but it's still a shock to the system when they're gone. I *knew* this was going to happen, but when it did I couldn't believe it. It was too much to take in. Too frightening. Too surreal.

The newsreader continued on, jumping from one report to another and relaying the information as soon as he got it. A breathless eyewitness from Hertfordshire stumbled and choked his way through a description of what could only have been an atomic explosion. He was cut off as he began asking what on earth we were going to do.

The newsreader had no answers for him. But what he did have, in fits and starts, were new reports. Of other explosions. Bristol. Manchester. Newcastle.

I had to get moving. I dove out into the rain, soaked to the bone the second I was out in the open. Rounding the back of the car I bent over, planting my arms on the boot for support as I gasped for breath. The enormity of the situation had blown my stage-by-stage mental preparation out of the window. My lungs felt tight and my head swiveled from left to right like a paranoid madman, lost and alone in a field of thick fog.

Focus, I thought. *You* must *focus or you* will *die. There's one chance to live, one chance!*

I fumbled with the latch, dove in too early and hit my head hard on the boot before it was fully open. I staggered backwards and fell into the sodden mud.

You are wasting time.

I got to my feet and lunged for my bags. There

were four of them in total, carefully thought out so that I could transport them to the boat without a return journey. A large rucksack for my back, a smaller one for my front, a large hold-all for one hand and most valuable of all, a solid, airtight plastic container for the other. There was also a headband with a powerful, waterproof flashlight attached to it, for my head.

Although the baggage was well planned, the weight surprised me. When I'd loaded the car, I'd done so one bag at a time. They'd all been heavy and I hadn't considered the difficulty of trying to carry them all at once. But then this ridiculous, spur of the moment plan was bound to have holes. I just hoped they wouldn't cost me the ultimate goal.

You are wasting time.

The journey to the boat wasn't far, but it was down a slippery path carved into the cliff. I went slow, picking my steps carefully by the light from my headlamp. I was concentrating so hard on my footing that I barely noticed the strong wind blowing in from the ocean. A fall or a bag lost over the side now would be devastating to the plan.

I had to stop twice for breath on the way, but I made it safely to the boat. It wasn't a large vessel, a simple mid-size wooden dinghy with a small motor, but it was all I'd been able to get my hands on in such a short space of time. It would just about accommodate my bags, myself and the two jerry cans full of diesel that I'd stashed in it earlier.

I'd tethered the boat to a metal spike driven into the mixture of large pebbles and filthy sand. It was already halfway into the water, so I could push it, laden with my possessions, out to sea without aid. And just as I was about to do so, I had a thought: *The car!*

I raced back up the path, frustrated at my lack of forethought. I couldn't leave any trace that I was here. It was too risky. If anyone noticed my abandoned car on the cliff, they may well trace it back to me or catch on to my idea. It was a leap and I was being paranoid, but I was alone in near pitch darkness, scrabbling around in the rain desperate for survival. And besides, these were paranoid times.

I reached the car, turned the steering wheel to full lock and released the handbrake. The car pitched to the left and lurched over the cliff. The bang as it hit the rocks and exploded was deafening in the darkness. I covered my ears and looked around wildly, for signs of life. There were none, but even in this remote outpost, that kind of noise could have been heard by someone in a nearby village or farmhouse. This thought jolted me out of my shock and I ran back to the path.

Back at the boat, I took a final glance towards the cliffs, now well illuminated by the blaze from the wreck of the car. There was no one peering down at me, no headlights or flashing sirens. If the totaled car was ever noticed by anyone, they would assume it had been driven over the cliff by accident (or on purpose), the driver dead. When they found no body they would suppose that it was perhaps, washed away by a high tide.

I untied the dinghy, dragged it out into the freezing water and climbed aboard. The motor started on the second pull and I steered the craft out, bumping over the crests and troughs of the tide and onward to the open sea.

3

I'd always celebrated my birthdays alone. In fact, *celebrated* is too strong a word. *Marked* would be more appropriate. *Took note of*, in the way we notice a change in the season, a chill in the night air as autumn approaches. Nothing to get too worked up about. A small glass of vodka to note the occasion perhaps. Just three days short of my thirty-third birthday, the intention was to be alone again. But this time under very different circumstances.

With the coastline falling away behind me, I reached into my jacket and pulled out a small GPS device, wrapped in a zip-lock bag. I had keyed in the coordinates during daylight but now the display, with its all important information, was hard to see in the dark. The flashlight on my headband glared off the plastic wrapper, but if I didn't look directly at it then I couldn't make anything out at all. I dared not remove the bag as the device wasn't waterproof and in addition to the relentless rain, the spray from the ocean was coming up from all sides of the boat.

I put it back in my pocket and reached for the headlamp, changing it to a reduced setting. The effect was immediate and frightening. I could barely see the front of the boat, let alone anything in front of it. Pitch black night surrounded me on every side. Suddenly the sound of the sea crashing around me seemed amplified to the level of a rock concert. It overwhelmed me and in pure instinct, I switched the flashlight back to full beam.

Much like waking from a childhood nightmare, the light brought an immediate sense of relief and safety. The raw fear brought about by the sudden dark was gone, but it took a second for the feeling to seep away. Plus my body was almost shaking from the adrenaline racing through it. I felt out of control and teetered on the edge of a full-blown panic attack. I tried to take some deep breaths and think it through.

Without the GPS I would drift off course, but without the headlamp on full beam I could run into something and wreck the boat. The further I got out to sea, the less chance of hitting any rocks, but a simple buoy would be enough to sink my little craft. My goal was a tiny dot on the map to the far north-west of the Scottish coast and there was nothing beyond it but miles and miles of open ocean. My fuel was limited and missing it was not an option.

I reasoned that the only choice I had was to check the GPS periodically. With one hand occupied steering the boat, the other would have to adjust the flashlight, take the GPS out, check it, put it away again and return the headlamp to full beam. This would make what I estimated to be about an eight hour journey, even longer.

As if to emphasise the problem, on first check I was already headed off course. Frustration and despair mixed themselves into a cocktail, with me and my boat the ice cubes being shaken and rattled around in the middle. *If only I'd had longer to plan*, I thought. And not for the first time. Two days planning while on the run was never going to be enough for an idea this far-fetched.

I released the throttle and let the motor sputter in the water. I retrieved some gaffer tape from the hold-all and tore off some strips, hanging them off the seat in front of me. Without the engine driving the boat forward, the swell of the sea felt more pronounced.

Everything about this plan relied on the GPS and I proceeded with extreme caution. It took several attempts, struggling for balance and trying to time my movements with the rise and fall of the sea. Finally, I managed to hold the unit in place with my chin and tape it to my forearm.

With the GPS unit in place, I could steer the boat, adjust the headlamp and check my heading more frequently. Satisfied with the solution, I grabbed the motor and proceeded full speed ahead again, out into the dark open waters of the North Atlantic.

As the shoreline faded into the shadows behind me, the enormity of what I was trying to do hit home. Here I was alone in this little boat, in the middle of a vast expanse of icy sea, being pelted by rain and thrown about by ever increasing swells. What on earth was I thinking?

I had spent so much effort focusing on the basics of the plan; where to go and when, what to take and how. It never sunk in that this bit, the simple matter of getting from A to B, was anything but. As the winds picked up and the ferocity of the sea grew, the stark question of whether my small vessel could even handle these conditions planted itself in my mind. I hadn't really considered it. I needed a boat urgently and this was the only one I could lay my hands on and the only one I could afford. The mental cycle I'd clung to, a mantra of going through my plan stage by stage, was blown apart and I felt the poison of fear seeping back into my veins.

How ironic to crash blindly into suicide in an attempt to avoid certain death. But the perfect irony of the situation saved me from turning around, heading back to the shore and backing out of the plan. Fear of death and self-preservation are deep biological programs. Although turning back felt less risky, I knew it meant certain death. Carrying on was also risky, but there was a chance of survival. When there are no good options, the more certain threat to life will always trump the next.

As I continued on, big surges would come and pitch the boat by forty-five degrees or more. The stab of panic each time was almost paralysing. That feeling of helplessness, of mercy to the elements, even overpowered my basic instincts such as breathing. I held my breath again and again as we roiled around. Sometimes the pitch was so sudden that I lost hold of the motor, causing the boat to swing violently in whatever way the current decreed. I floundered around in desperation until I found it again, forced a deep breath and reset the course.

In spite of the gnawing fear, with each small victory over a wave, with each near-death experience survived, I grew minutely in confidence. After a couple of hours I began to feel that maybe this could be done, if I could just keep going. As I hurdled a lumpy surge front-on and rode down into the trough, I smiled for the briefest of moments. It was the smile of a person losing their grip on sanity. But it didn't matter. I was doing this. It was going to work.

'Come on you bastard!' I roared in challenge to the ocean.

And it responded in kind, hitting the boat side-on with the biggest wave yet and launching me over the side, into the freezing depths.

4

The number said unknown, but I knew exactly who the text message had come from the moment I received it.

"Check your email."

It was Friday, mid-morning and I was standing in the kitchen on the second floor of the building where I worked when the phone buzzed in my pocket. It was a small and functional space, more of a corridor than a room, with no doors on either side and just a thin wall separating it from the rest of the open-plan office. Not much chance of privacy, but nothing strange either, about a person checking their phone while the coffee brewed.

Except that it was strange to me. Because it was my personal phone, not my work one. And nobody had that number.

It was such a short space of time between everything feeling normal and the world coming to the brink of apocalypse. No more than a week. One day I was headed off to work on a dreary Monday morning and just a few days later, triggered by a seemingly innocuous text, I was frantically formulating a survival plan.

In reality though, the desperate situation had been building for many years. Some might say it had started with the widespread election of increasingly fringe politicians to the pinnacle of power around the world. But I would disagree. These people had gained power for a reason. The warning signs had been there, we'd just missed them.

In the media, these shock results from several worldwide elections had been blamed on a rise in populism. Traditional parties and politicians all over the world were being ousted in favour of more right-wing, nationalistic ones. These types either truly believed their isolationist policies or had spotted an opportunity to gain power, and adopted the necessary hyperbole to win.

This was nothing new to the world of course. But the rapid growth and success of such politics in what we considered 'modern times', was. And there was a reason behind that too.

The gap between rich and poor had been growing for many years. The middle classes were being eroded. For the vast majority of people, life was getting harder. Disposable incomes were disappearing and people were working to survive, with less and less reward. Politicians in general felt secure in their high salaries and good prospects and began to lose touch with the struggles of the average person on the street. Although they talked a good game (and to the credit of some of them, really did try to ease the burden), through a lack of understanding and a desire to remain in their positions, their policies missed the mark.

A large majority of people were struggling and because of that, they were angry and scared. Several years of just getting by, ever fearful of an unexpected expense or a loss of income, took their toll. When such fear pervades everyday life, year after year, so that it becomes the norm for the majority of society, the voices of strong rhetoric and blame begin to be heard, no matter how misguided. People became desperate. They lost faith in their governments. They began to listen to anyone who offered an alternative.

And that is perhaps, where it all started. In the mighty countries of the world, politicians who would have been considered to be on the periphery in recent history, swept to power on a wave of anger and consolidated their positions with isolationist policies. This on its own, may not have led to the end. But these men knew their power was based on strong, uncompromising and intolerant virtues. And when a small middle-eastern trade route was disrupted by a civil war in the region, rationality and diplomacy was lost in a sea of tough-talk and propaganda. World leaders on opposite sides of opinion painted themselves into a corner, refusing to back down for fear of appearing weak and losing the support of their base.

The initial disagreement escalated into full scale threats. While more independent countries such as China tried to mediate, others were forced to pick sides. The airwaves became saturated with angry political diatribe. Military exercises were performed in competing nation's backyards. Airspaces were intruded upon. Troop movements were made. Finally, a line in the sand was drawn. An ultimatum with a deadline by which if one nation did not remove its forces from along a border, the other would be forced to act.

But the world had seen this kind of political posturing before. The rapid escalation and subsequent de-escalation of hostilities was common in recent memory. In contrast, the devastation of two global conflicts had happened far enough in the past that no one currently living had experienced them. Or more importantly, had experienced what had led the world to war in the first place. So nobody really believed it would happen. Myself included.

Two days before I received the text message, I'd been at my desk eating lunch. I read about the deadline on a news website, in an article with the headline "World at Brink". At midnight on Sunday either one side would back down, or the world would pay the consequences.

The Doomsday Clock, a symbolic warning to the world of impending man-made global catastrophe, had been set to thirty seconds to midnight. The clock had been created in the aftermath of the second world war and this was the closest it had been set to midnight in history. *Just thirty seconds to save the world* it said. But the metaphor fell on deaf ears.

Reading that article is when it became real to me. A genuine threat of global meltdown. I still couldn't entertain the idea that the world could end.

But the nature of the deadline put me on edge.

Russia had massed forces along the border of the Black Sea, within striking distance of a U.S. military base in Bulgaria. They claimed it was merely a defensive measure, but the President of the United States saw it as a direct challenge. He had issued an ultimatum: move the forces away from the Black Sea by midnight on Sunday June 13th or America would be forced into a preemptive attack.

I had studied the Cuban Missile Crisis in school, where the world was brought to the edge of nuclear conflict by a similar ultimatum. But this time it felt different. More dangerous somehow. This wasn't a case of warships far out in international waters, this was military forces in their own country.

I thought of the story of Lieutenant Colonel Stanislav Petrov, the Russian man who had saved the world from Nuclear conflict in 1983. Three weeks after the Soviet shooting down of a Korean passenger jet, he had received an alert from the nuclear early warning system, of multiple missile launches from the U.S. He had judged them to be a false alarm. That judgement and his subsequent breach of protocol, had prevented an erroneous retaliation which would have led to a third world war. I wondered if we would be so lucky this time.

I worried about it, but I didn't lose any sleep over it. Like others, I reasoned that the world had come a long way since then. Rational heads would surely prevail.

It was only when I got the text that I realised they wouldn't.

5

After reading the message, I went back to my desk and sat staring at the blank monitor in front of me, my coffee forgotten. In a panic held just beneath my skin, I tried to think straight and consider my options.

I tapped at the keyboard and clicked the mouse from time to time to make it look like I was working. But I couldn't concentrate. I looked at my watch: 11.30am. Five and a half hours before I could leave. Another forty-five minutes before I was home. Ten more to move the wardrobe, peel back the wallpaper and retrieve the laptop from its hiding place in an alcove carved out of the wall. Altogether that was six hours and forty minutes before I could check the email. Too long.

My commute was too far to get home and back over lunch. If the email said what I thought it might, I wouldn't be coming back that afternoon anyway, but I had to be cautious. If I was wrong about this, or if anything steered humanity away from this dreadful course, I needed to be able to come back to work on Monday, with no questions asked.

I decided to rely on my exemplary record and 100% attendance rate. I asked my boss for a quiet word and feigned an illness.

'Something in my stomach,' I said. 'It came on last night but I felt ok this morning and thought I could manage it.'

He was very sympathetic and I felt guilt at the genuine empathy on his face.

'Please go home,' he said. 'We can manage without you this afternoon, I'm sure.' I returned his smile and thanked him. I tried not to look rushed as I gathered my belongings and left.

It was the middle of the day and there were plenty of seats available on the underground, but I remained standing for the whole journey. I was too anxious to sit. I looked at the faces around me and wondered if they were as worried as I was. Did they have any idea what was happening? Or were they too wrapped up in their virtual bubbles? How would they react if the worst happened?

I'd seen the post apocalypse films and TV shows. Although I believed that the darker side of humanity was always played up for the purposes of dramatization, I also knew that when people became desperate, they did desperate things. If the world faced a global conflict then food would be scarce. It would happen slowly at first, but as people began to notice the empty supermarket shelves, the panic would set in. A nuclear conflict would be even worse. Instant chaos and devastation in every major city. With a vacuum of power, resources disappearing and law and order failing, there was a very real chance that society would collapse. Nowhere would be safe.

Nowhere would be safe. At the end of that thought was when the idea came to me, at first just a wistful notion.

There might be one unique type of place that would be safe. I remembered an article I'd read about the most isolated places on earth. Tristan da Cunha, more than 3,000 miles from the coast of South Africa, had been number one on the list. Although about as far from civilisation as possible, there was a population of 200 who lived there year in, year out.

That was beyond my meagre means, but there was another island I'd heard about in a nature documentary, far to the North West of Scotland, which could be in reach. It was called St. Rita and was populated up until the late 1960's, when the aging inhabitants, struggling with various health issues, left for the mainland and never returned.

I remembered seeing pictures of it. There were buildings on the island, now abandoned but very much intact. There was rudimentary infrastructure that remained; a dilapidated dock and a large building by a helipad, with a clear plastic roof that had a humorous sign outside designating it as the 'airport lounge'. Although the roof had a fair amount of damage, it gave me an idea which could prove crucial to survival.

There were no boats or aircraft which went there anymore. But up until the late 1980's there had been a regular boat trip for tourists who wanted to camp on the island and do some birdwatching. So it must have been reachable.

If I could make it there,' I thought, *perhaps I could survive.* At the very least, with those old buildings there, I wouldn't be starting from scratch.

The stations continued to rattle by one by one, the journey through the underground seeming to take far too long.

6

The shock of the freezing water numbed my senses and blew the air from my lungs. I flapped my arms about and gasped for breath, acting on raw instinct. Conscious thought was not possible.

In these first few valuable seconds, with the dinghy still within reach, I was like a young child exposed to water for the first time, thrashing around with inefficient strokes and swallowing gallons of salty water. Every part of my body and brain was focused on managing to keep my head above the water. There was no thought, only action.

An electric moment of clarity struck me, ripping me from the grip of the icy shock. *You are alone in the middle of the ocean. And your boat is drifting away.*

I swung my head around trying to see but the darkness was impenetrable. I could feel the pitch-black water rise and fall around me but I couldn't see it. I grasped my forehead but the headlight was gone. I looked down in the purest moment of panic I have ever felt, vainly hoping to spot it sinking to the depths and rescue it.

There was a glow around my neck, just beneath the water. The fall had forced the headlamp down over my head but the strap was still around my neck. I ripped it up over my ears and secured it back on my forehead.

My eyes took another valuable moment away from me, as they adjusted to the light and I blinked to clear the stinging water away. There was nothing but a dark wall of ocean in front of me.

A swell picked me up, the current floating me to its highest point. And there, mercifully, I spotted the boat, a few metres away in the trough. I lunged for it, kicking as hard as I could in my heavy, sodden clothing. As the wave passed I was hurtled downwards toward the craft and had to duck under the water, lest the side struck my head and knocked me out.

I reached up and grasped around the hull, desperate for purchase. But the need to breathe overcame me and I had to push myself back out and struggle away to the surface.

Another swell came and separated me again from my life raft. With everything I had, I worked against the current. The front of the boat began to turn away from me and as we once more sailed together into the trough, the propeller came rushing towards my face. With my arms and legs stroking hard, I railed against the invisible pull of the ocean. It was so strong that I couldn't force myself away from the boat, only slow my progress toward it. The boat continued to turn and I gave one final, massive backwards heave against the heavy drag of the wash. The blades passed an inch away from my face.

I leaned into the water and kicked out, driving myself in the opposite direction that the boat was turning, until the side of it was in front of me. I lunged for it, a desperate arm striking upwards for salvation. My hand gripped the slippery gunwale and I held on for dear life.

Reaching the boat was one thing. Getting back in it was another entirely. I managed to get my other hand onto the side, but every time I tried to haul myself in the weight of my body and sodden clothes wouldn't tip the boat enough to swing a leg in, but was too much to lift myself up enough to lean into the hull.

I tried again and again without success, my muscles more fatigued and my mind more numb with cold with every attempt. But having hold of the boat had given me some reassurance and my mind had settled just enough for coherent thought.

I maneuvered the craft slowly around by kicking my legs, until it was in front of me with the current behind. As the next swell came I rode up with it. Just before the boat lurched upwards I lunged, with just enough force to get my top half over the edge. I grasped the seat and pulled with all my might, flailing my legs out until my soaking body was completely out of the water and into the boat.

I lay there on top of my belongings for several minutes, breathing hard and gripping the sides as the boat bobbed up and down. Staring up at the dark blank sky, I thanked a god I didn't believe in. For helping me get back on board and for my headlight being waterproof. Had I bought it for that reason? I couldn't remember. But I thanked god that it was.

When my body and senses finally recovered enough to get upright and back into my place in front of the engine, I sat there shivering with my head in my hands. It was all too much. I had to go back.

But back to what? I asked myself. British cities would not be the only ones hit and even if Scotland escaped assault, the nuclear fallout would spread across the whole island. Millions would die. The government would collapse. If anyone remained, society would still descend into hell.

No, I had got this far, had done all this for a reason. To make it to safety, to survive. What good would it do to return and die anyway. Pushing on was the only choice I had. From a deep reserve I didn't know I had, I summoned enough perseverance to fortify myself.

'Come on,' I said out loud, willing myself into action. 'COME. ON.'

Reinvigorated, at least mentally, I fired up the engine and got the boat moving. Then I looked down at the GPS and my heart sank again, this time to the very bottom of the sea. It was still strapped to my arm, but the zip lock bag I'd placed around it was long gone. Unlike the headlamp it was not waterproof. It was dead.

7

I hurtled up the stairs to my first floor apartment and drove the key into the lock. I hesitated for a moment before opening the door, my eyes ferreting around and my ears straining for the hint of anything unusual. Footsteps behind me. A van idling too close to the building. Anything that might indicate that I was being watched or followed. It was stupid, I knew it was stupid, but my heart was beating faster than a driving rain, surging my paranoia like static through my veins. A single drop of sweat trickled down behind my ear and onto the back of my neck.

Nothing. There was no one behind me or above me on the stairs and nothing other than the sound of the neighbour's dog barking outside. That dog was always barking. Nothing unusual about that.

I flung the door open hard, to catch anyone standing behind it by surprise. It swung back on its hinges and made a loud bang against the wall. I stepped inside and closed it behind my back, keeping my line of sight on the living room of the apartment in front of me.

It was a scarce space. Two mismatched old armchairs sat in front of an old cathode-ray TV set, perched on the rickety stand it probably came with. There was no other furniture, no pictures on the walls and nothing but a beige plastic blind pulled halfway up the window. I walked over to it, pulled the string and let it crash all the way down to the windowsill. There were no rugs on the floor and the echo from the heels of my office shoes clapping against the wooden floor, reverberated a hollow sound around the off-white walls of the apartment.

I stood by the now covered window, listening again for any signs of life in the apartment. There were none. *There never is,* I thought. *Even when I'm home.*

I slipped my shoes off and made my way to the short corridor at the end of the room. Three doors, all shut, just as I had left them. The first one on the left opened to a tiny kitchen, more of a cupboard than an actual room. Nothing in there but a small fridge, single hob and rusty old kettle. The second led to a slightly bigger and immaculately clean, but no more than functional, bathroom. The final door on the right, was the entrance to the only bedroom. That was the room that held the laptop that I had rushed home to use.

I crouched down in front of the door and pushed it open, ready to launch up at anyone lurking inside. I had done the same thing a hundred times, but this time felt different. The need to be prepared somehow more urgent, because of the text message.

Inside the room there was a small double bed

opposite an old, brown chest of drawers. There was no one inside. I stood up and walked in, my eyes locking on the wardrobe in the far corner, the only piece of furniture in the apartment that was neither cheap nor faded. It was a heavy oak affair, solidly built with three sections. It was completely impractical for the small room and a beast to move, but that was the point. Storing my few outfits was only it's secondary purpose.

I opened the first door and planted my hands inside against the wall of the wardrobe. I braced for the strain and then pushed hard, using jerky movements to shift it forward away from the corner of the room. Once there was a foot or so between it and the wall, I closed the door and moved to the space in-between.

Behind the wardrobe the wall was lined with a textured wallpaper, the same colour as the walls in the rest of the apartment. I tugged at the bottom corner of the wallpaper and the hidden velcro strip which held it in place gave way. I peeled it back carefully, all the way off until it leant against the wardrobe. There, concealed behind it and flat to the wall, was a small white cabinet which would look like an old fuse box to an untrained eye. I reached up and opened the cabinet grasping the small black laptop stood on its end inside.

I sat on the bed with the laptop balanced on my knees and fired it up. It loaded to a flat black screen, a single white cursor pulsing in the top left corner. I typed in a long series of letters and numbers from memory and slapped the enter key. The screen flashed:

`Incorrect password`

I typed the series of letters and numbers in again, with the same result. After the third attempt the text on the screen warned me that I had run out of tries and the laptop was now locked and would require a system administrator to unlock it.

I hit ctrl, shift, escape and a cursor appeared again beneath the warning message. I typed in the same series of letters and numbers again.

The screen cleared and a series of white dots appeared one after the other across the screen, followed by a number of messages which flashed once and then disappeared.

`IP Verified`

`VPN enabled`

`Rerouting`

Finally the screen cleared again and a single link appeared with the words "New Message" flashing beside it. I clicked the link.

The message was just two lines long. I read it three times to be sure I hadn't misunderstood anything. Then I lay back onto the bed, the laptop crashing to the floor, and stared at the ceiling, tears forming in my eyes.

8

After multiple attempts at drying, tapping and shaking and the GPS to no avail, I sat staring out into the darkness around me. The rain had lightened, but still came down in a drizzle that was as relentless as my situation was depressing. Even if I wanted to go back now, without the GPS I wouldn't know the way.

As I bobbed up and down and side to side in the little boat, my mind emptied. The short relief I felt when I made it back on-board had been replaced by a deep despair. My brain had gone for the only option it had left to keep me sane: it had switched off entirely.

For more than an hour I floated, engine off, no thoughts in my head, indifferent to the battering of the wind and spray from the ocean.

A jolt from a particularly big wave caused me to grasp the seat instinctively. The memory of the icy shock and panic from plunging into the water made its way back to me through the mental fog. I was stuck somewhere in the ocean with no idea which way to go.

I could simply switch the engine on, point the boat in one direction and go. But get it wrong, head due west for example, and there would be nothing but miles and miles of hungry North Atlantic sea to greet me.

The darkness too, meant that I wouldn't spot any unlikely tract of land that could save me. And there were no lighthouses out this far.

I cast my eyes about in search of an answer. With nothing but sea and darkness outside the boat, I began looking at each of my bags in turn, taking a mental inventory in the hope of inspiration. I had many of the things I thought would come in handy to survive on the island, but nothing that would help me get there.

With no other ideas however, I continued cycling through the bags from largest to smallest, listing the contents in my head. I got to the smallest, the backpack I'd carried down the cliff on my chest. Inside was day one essentials; a change of clothes, a couple of tins, a can opener and fork, some fire starting implements and a flask of coffee.

A flask of coffee, I thought. What was I expecting? A pleasant journey on smooth seas with time for a quick brew on the way? Ha! Despite my grim situation, a weary smile touched my lips at the thought.

I stared down at the full-to-bursting pack. It was a professional climbers backpack, not quite waterproof but sturdy nonetheless. It would serve a day traveler well, with its ample space, comfortable straps and numerous pockets on the front and sides.

The pockets. It hit me hard. I had to fight the drive to tear them open and spill their contents onto the deck. I couldn't remember which one I'd stashed my phone in, but it wouldn't do to rip one open and accidentally launch it over the side.

With forced carefulness and deliberate motions, I opened first the left side, then the right. Nothing. But when I opened the front pocket, there in another zip lock bag was my smartphone.

I remembered now. I had charged it fully, switched it off and stored it in plastic to protect it from the elements. I'd done so *just in case.* Just in case I made it to the island and heard on the radio that somehow, all was not lost. Just in case there was a signal and I could send a text to someone, begging for rescue. At the time it had been an afterthought, something to fill the painstaking last few hours of waiting. But now it meant everything.

I removed the bag and powered it on with numbed fingers. I couldn't make a call this far out to sea but the GPS locator might still work, the way it does on a plane sometimes. I hit the maps icon and held my breath as it loaded. *If this doesn't work…*

After processing for a few seconds, the application opened. The last thing I'd searched for, another merciful coincidence, was the island. There it was, in all it's two dimensional glory. And there, several miles to the south, was a little blue dot which indicated my position.

I whooped to the night sky, pumping my fist. I had drifted far to the West on the current, but if I headed North, the island would eventually appear.

I ripped the GPS unit off my arm and grabbed the tape to replace it with the phone. Then I thought better of it and decided to tape the phone to the seat in front of me instead, just in case I fell overboard again.

All I needed now was to head North. I looked out to the sea again, swinging my head from left to right. Which way was North? I looked up to the sky, with a vague notion of finding the North Star. There were no stars tonight however. The cloud cover was as dark and menacing as the sea.

I looked back at the phone. I could periodically check my direction of travel I supposed, making corrections as I went. That might work. *I don't suppose…* I scrolled through the list of apps and there it was. A compass. Another small victory!

I tapped on the settings and set the screen to permanently on, fired up the engine and pointed the boat in a North Easterly direction, trying to take account of the strong Western current. Once again I was on my way. Back to navigating the rolling waters. Back to bracing myself for each peak and trough.

I began to feel exhilarated again. It was a tempered excitement; the type a child may feel running again to the fairground, after tripping and falling the first time. But it was a positive feeling all the same. This *could* work. I *could* make it.

The going felt slow. Each time I checked the map I had to make an adjustment. I was generally traveling to the North, but either the current or my over-adjustments kept taking me off course. At times I was drifting too far West and others too far East. As long as the blue dot continued to inch ever upwards however, I was on the right track.

After several hours the rain had all but stopped, the wind had softened and the sea had begun to settle. It was still a bumpy ride, but I no longer feared capsizing or being swept overboard by a rogue wave.

Perhaps there will be time for a coffee after all. I smiled at this silly thought and checked the phone again. My smile turned to a grimace. The little green indicator which signified a healthy battery had turned to a sickly amber. 35%. Would it be enough?

I resolved to turn the screen off in-between checks and reduced the brightness as far as I could. In the darkness of the night and with nothing but my head lamp to disturb it, the screen was still readable at a low setting.

I didn't want to even consider what would happen if the battery ran out. I blocked the thought from entering my head and increased the speed of the vessel.

9

I crashed on through the night, checking my phone in ever decreasing intervals as the battery ran down. I was getting closer, but not close enough.

The rain started up again, falling in a light drizzle. It wasn't too troublesome, but still substantial enough to keep my clothes thoroughly soaked. The wind remained calm, but damp as I was and with my nerves shattered, a shiver continued to drive through me. My teeth chattered even when I clamped my jaw shut.

After hours at sea my mind had reached an oblivious state. My command of the boat had become almost a second nature and my only thought was of reaching the island. I put the dying battery to the back of mind, telling myself that *I would make it* and *It can't be much further.*

But as I checked the map and set my compass heading for the last time, a loading circle came up and then the phone went dead. There was no way to ignore it anymore.

I looked over the rim of the boat and up at the sky, with the idea of fixing a point to follow that would at least keep me heading in the right general direction. But there was nothing there except the empty ocean and a thick layer of grey cloud above it.

Grey cloud. I could *see* the texture of the clouds now. They were dim, but I could see them. I'd been in such a trance that the slow rise of daylight had crept up on me. It was a small boost which brought me back to my senses. At least now, if I continued to head in the right direction, I would not miss the island if it appeared on the horizon.

I pushed on. What choice did I have? The sun rose, not that I could see it for the overcast sky, and the temperature rose a little with it. The chattering and shivering ceased. It wasn't *warm* in my little vessel but whether it was the return of the sun or the hope of daybreak, I *felt* warmer.

And then, an hour or so later, it happened.

As my anxiousness about my heading reached a fever pitch, I cast my eyes left to right across the horizon, desperate for sight of anything but the sea. A rock, a loose buoy, anything would do. And there it was, a dim shadow off to my far right. I could barely make it out, but unless I was hallucinating that dark shape was unmistakably an island.

I swerved the boat towards it, half-standing to get a better view. I had never felt such elation in all my life. Driven half mad by the journey, I shouted 'Land ho!' over and over again, until my throat was raw.

Had it not been for the rising sun and my good fortune in scouring about the horizon when I did, I would have missed it. But there it was, plain as day. A wave of relief washed over me, tinged with a deep disbelief that I was almost there. The doubts about what came next circled around the back of my mind like snakes slithering over each other in a ditch, but as the island grew ever larger in front of me, it didn't matter. I was going to make it. I would be safe. If only for a few hours.

The Island of St Rita was bigger than I had expected, with a large, steep hill to one side which sloped down to flatter ground and a small bay on the other. As I approached I could make out a line of small grey stone buildings a short way up from the shore. The thought of being inside again was like the sight of ice cold water to a man with a hot and avid thirst.

After hour upon hour of black skies and dark water, I was taken aback by how green the island was. I'd seen the pictures online, but they didn't do it justice. In my mind I had pictured only the unforgiving and rocky landscape, grey and imposing from the sea. Not the beautiful, wavy, light-green grass that covered the slope of the island, all the way up to the cliffs at the top. Nor the crystal clear water in the tiny, shallow bay.

I ignored the dilapidated wooden dock which reached like a skeletal arm out from one side of the bay. I aimed the dinghy straight for the beach instead. I wanted to be on land more than anything I had ever wanted before. I floored the gas and headed hard toward the centre of the pebble strewn shore.

I didn't slow at all, instead bracing for impact as the ground rushed towards me. As the front of the boat hit solid ground, it was launched into the air. Not by much, as laden down as it was, but enough to get it clear of the water by a good half a metre or so. I tumbled forward, smacking my head on the seat in front of me. The pain only existed outside of a void though and I jumped from the boat and grabbed the rope tied to the bow. With a strength I didn't know I had left in me, I tossed the rope over my shoulder and hefted the raft further up the bay. I didn't know how far the tide came in, but judging by the seaweed and other flotsam, I'd pulled it far enough.

I collapsed onto my back beside the boat and lay staring up at the clouds. I'd done it. The first part of the plan had worked. Everything had gone wrong and I'd almost drowned, but I'd made it.

The morning light stung my eyes so I closed them. And within seconds I slipped into a deep sleep, right there on the shore.

It would be the last sound sleep I had for many months.

10

I woke a couple of hours later with a start. My head was throbbing and my body ached like it had been infected with a crippling dose of flu. I blinked at the sky and wiped my eyes, unsure for a second, of exactly where I was. The rain had stopped but the clouds remained, grey and ominous as ever.

You're on the island. The thought brought with it all the suppressed anxiety that I'd pushed away during my struggle on the sea. This was the moment that it all felt very real for the first time. I was alone in the middle of nowhere. There were no shops, no hospitals, no electricity. No one was coming to help. I had made it, but now I had to survive out here.

Deal with things in stages, I thought. *One thing at a time.*

The first task was to empty the boat and carry my belongings up the shore and into one of the old buildings. *Shelter. One of the core needs of survival.* The rest were water, food, air and sleep. The air was clean and

I had food and water in my bags. More sleep could wait. Shelter was the priority.

I rose gingerly, my head banging a drumbeat to match my every movement. One by one I lifted my bags over the side, taking extra care over the sealed cool-box. I arranged them about myself just as I had done the night before, which seemed so very long ago now. With slow, heavy steps I hefted them up towards the scattering of abandoned buildings.

The first door I came to was locked. I couldn't believe it. Surely one of the last things you might do when abandoning a building was lock the door? I walked further up and tried the second. Mercifully, it opened and I stumbled inside.

I kicked it shut behind me and then offloaded my bags one by one. It was dark and dusty inside but a dim light seemed to follow my line of vision as I glanced around. Wherever I looked it appeared in front of me on the nearest surface. My tired, confused brain took a minute to work out that this was my headlamp, running low on power now, but still working.

I switched it off and took in my surroundings. The walls and floor were simple stone and there were a couple of puddles on the floor where the roof had leaked. There was a kitchen area to my right, all its cupboards open and bare. In front of me and just to my left, I was surprised to see an old wooden table and six chairs which looked like they belonged in a boarding school for orphans, stood near a fireplace on the far wall. Well, I suppose when you're transferring all your worldly goods by boat and there's no need to empty a place, you might leave some of the older, heavier furniture behind.

At the front of the house and on the right-hand wall of the kitchen were glass windows, each of them made of small squares of glass in a six-piece frame. I was pleased to see that only one of these had broken. All of the rest were intact.

Right, you're inside. Stages. What is the next step?

I was cold, damp and thirsty. Despite all I had been through, it was still morning and the desire for caffeine was strong. I decided to change into some dry clothes and think through my next steps while I nursed a coffee.

I retrieved an old hoodie and some tracksuit bottoms from my hold-all and arranged my sodden clothes onto the backs of the chairs to dry. It looked a mess, but there were no guests to worry about here. Once changed and dry I removed the thermos from my backpack and sat at the table facing the windows as I poured myself a drink.

The coffee was still lukewarm, which was far more than I'd expected. I drank the first cup down in one gulp and poured another. My head still banged, making it hard to think. I'd stashed some painkillers in a small first aid kit along with some bandages, antiseptic cream, tape and whatever other over-the-counter drugs I'd been able to get. I grabbed a couple of pills and swallowed them, before resting my head on my hands and waiting for the drugs to kick in.

Now dry and with caffeine and paracetamol flowing through me, my head began to clear and I felt able to think again. I sipped at the rest of the coffee and went back to trying to think in stages. It was late-morning already. I knew I needed to recce the island as soon as possible, but didn't feel up to it at that point. The journey had taken so much out of me and physically I was exhausted.

Ok, I thought;

Step one: explore the rest of this dwelling.

Step two: prepare for immediate survival, identify meals for the next one-two days

Step three: explore the other buildings and make an inventory of anything in them

Step four: Arrange living quarters

That would do for now.

I looked out the window, delaying getting up until I felt strong enough. It was still overcast. Opposite the dwelling was a rock wall half a metre high on the other side of the path. It blocked the view of the shoreline, but I could see the sea and hear it crashing against the rocks below. It was the only sound I could hear. It hit me again: I was alone. There was no one around me for miles and miles.

The thought spurred me to my feet.

11

Just keep busy.

I thought if I kept my mind focused on each task at hand, then I wouldn't have time to think about where I was and what I was doing. And not thinking about *that* felt very important.

Stage one was to explore the rest of the dwelling, so that's what I did. In addition to the two open-plan front rooms, there was a small, short corridor leading out from the back wall. Halfway down the corridor on the left hand side, was a doorway into what I assumed was a bedchamber, although there was no furniture in it. The right hand side of the corridor was just solid, grey stone but there was a closed door at the end. I opened it and was back outside.

There was an area of overgrown flora out the back, surrounded by a dilapidated, low stone wall which had completely given way in some sections. Immediately to the left as I came out the door was a small cubed section of the house with a door to the side. Odd.

I opened this door and it all made sense. In front of me, in a poor and dirty state of repair was a rusty handheld shower hose, plumbed directly into the wall, and a toilet. I hadn't given that much thought, but I guess the old inhabitants had to go somewhere.

I reached out almost on instinct and pulled the lever that the shower head hung from. There was a choking sound, but nothing else. *Where would the water come from?*

I stepped back outside and looked up at the roof of the cubicle. There was something up there. I jumped up and grabbed the ledge, pulling myself up just enough to get a look at the top. It was built like a vast sink, with walls around the side and a basin which was filled with debris and a grim looking sludge. *To collect the rain.*

I added a step to the list, something further down for when I had more strength: clear the basin out and unclog the pipe.

Buoyed by this odd discovery, I headed back through my new home and out the front. Stage two was supposed to be setting out some meals and preparing for immediate survival, but I wanted to see what other nice surprises might be waiting for me in the other buildings.

I went back to the first building I'd come across, nearest the shore. Facing the front door I braced myself to kick it open. *Seems easy enough on the TV*, I thought.

I kicked it full force, but instead of swinging open, my foot went straight through it. The wood splintered in all different directions. The majority of the door remained in place. *Ok, not so easy.*

The jagged edges caught on my tracksuit bottoms and I struggled for balance as I freed myself. I stumbled backwards and felt a jagged edge tear a deep cut into my calf, right through the material wrapped around it. It wasn't serious, but it was my first lesson. *One slip, one foolish injury and it's over.* There would be others.

I got to my feet, reached up into the inside of the door and fumbled with the latch. The door opened into a building much the same as the last. It was another house, with the same room layout. Several of the windows had broken in this one however and the inside was damp and filthy. I looked around inside and was disappointed not to find anything left behind.

The first and second houses were joined together and there was a third further up. Guessing this would be the same, I decided to inventory it last and instead head up to another scattering of buildings I could see further up the island.

The slope from the shore continued upwards for another hundred yards and then crested out into a lopsided square with three buildings arranged facing opposite each other. Two of them were single story, but the one at the end was double and much bigger, so I went there first. It looked like a large farmhouse.

There was something eerie about venturing into these former homes. Although I was the only person on the island and the previous inhabitants had long since left them behind, it still felt like I was trespassing somehow. *There's no one here,* I kept reminding myself. But more than once I noticed I was creeping around, rather than boldly exploring.

The door to the big house was open but creaked so loudly on its hinges that I jumped. I hesitated to go in at first, instead glancing around for some sort of weapon. *Foolish. Just get on with it.*

I called out a forlorn 'Hello?' before going inside and the sound of my voice, breaking the white noise of the wind and sea, brought back forbidden thoughts of my situation again. *Keep busy.*

The house seemed even bigger on the inside. Unlike the smaller ones, instead of opening directly into the front rooms, the front door opened to a wide corridor which ended in a kitchen through a doorway at the back.

The first room on the left was a large square space, with a couple of dusty, broken armchairs pushed against one wall. Built out from the back wall on the right hand side was a collapsed wooden structure which looked very much like a small bar. *The bar at the end of the world,* I thought. *This must have been used as a meeting place for the islanders.*

I continued through the house. There were five other rooms, one empty one opposite the large room and four more up a wooden staircase which groaned all the way up. The kitchen at the end looked out onto another rundown garden and I noticed two further structures in the distance, which had been hidden from my view on approach. One looked very much like a barn with a big metal gate and the other was the plastic dome with a steel frame, which I remembered from the pictures. I would investigate these later, but for now I had found something of great value in the smallest bedroom.

There was no mattress, but the metal frame of the single bed looked to be in good shape. The wires which supported the frame were sharp and rusty but I thought I could make it work if I could find some wood to lie over it. One of the interior doors would do. I'd bought a toolkit with me and could unscrew one in no time.

A bed. An actual bed. I had brought a rollout camping mattress and sleeping bag with me of course, but I never considered that I might find such luxury! There were other buildings to investigate, but I was feeling positive and excited about my find. So I decided to move the bed back to my new home and return to stage two.

It took me deep into the afternoon to drag the stubborn, heavy bed frame out of the big house and down the hill. I had to stop several times to catch my breath. I was sweating profusely by the time I got it into what would be my bedroom from now on.

Once it was in place I headed back to the first house with my toolbox. From the outside its broken front door and windows gave it a sinister look. But it would be good for spare parts if nothing else. I made my way to the bedroom, intending to unscrew the door and use it as the base for my bed. But when I looked at the hinges, they were so rusted and broken that a couple of stiff tugs were enough to rip it off from the bracket.

I carried the unwieldy plank of wood back to the bed frame and tossed it on top. Then I rolled out my camping mattress over it and settled cautiously into a horizontal position on top. The springs creaked and the whole thing sunk half an inch or so, but it held my weight fine.

I lay there for a moment, staring up at the dark grey stone of the ceiling. The small window above me faced the steep back of the island and didn't let in much light. Exhausted from my exertions but too wired and thirsty to nap, my thoughts drifted to the cool-box sitting in the living room. I couldn't put it off forever. I would have to open it some time.

12

It's amazing how the most superfluous of items can seem like essentials in our lives. Our cars, our phones, our TV's – they all seem like things we couldn't live without. We take for granted the simple things that really are essential to our very existence. A flowing tap for example.

I had brought a good amount of water with me, enough I thought, to last a month or so if I rationed it. Enough to keep me going until I'd set up something more sustainable at least. I'd calculated that more than enough rain fell in these parts and if I could capture and store it somehow, then I'd be fine. I'd also bought an expensive salt water purifier pump from a camping store, but it would have to be a last resort. The effort it took to work the pump and desalinate the water would barely make it worth the amount I could produce to drink. If I tried to live off of it, I would slowly dehydrate anyway.

Driven by thirst, I'd finally risen from the ramshackle bed and downed an entire bottle of water.

Having drunk so much in one go, I realised that my considerable supply was not quite as considerable as I'd thought. I had shelter. Next on the list from the core survival needs would have to be water.

I thought about it while I sat at the table in the living room, spooning cold beans into my mouth straight from the can. I'd brought a camping stove, but I wanted to preserve the little gas canister for as long as I could. My mind turned to the previous inhabitants. I would need to start thinking more like them. They'd lived on this island for generations, what had they done for water?

It occurred to me that there must be some kind of well or water tower on the island. If there was then I would have to tour the island to find it, and soon. But what if they'd had a tower and it had been destroyed by a storm? Or if the well had run out or been contaminated? What would I do then?

One thing at a time. My mantra returned: *Stages.*

I had a few hours of daylight left and it had rained for several hours the night before. If I could find some sort of pool where it had collected, then that would be a start. Find somewhere the water collects naturally and store a bit of it - just as a temporary measure. But first I'd need something to collect it into.

I finished off the beans. I could use the tin to ferry the water into a bigger vessel if I had one. I looked at my cool-box. *Perfect. But that would mean opening it.*

I looked around my belongings for an alternative, but there wasn't one. Using the cool-box would mean having the valuable contents out in the open. It felt safer knowing they were all there in one place, protected from the elements. And one in particular, I didn't want to think about just now. Having it on show would make that unavoidable.

Stages. I decided to try and find a bucket or something similar first, while I went looking for a water source. If I couldn't find one, then I could always come back for the cool-box. Conscious that the rain had stopped a while ago and the longer it lay out in a ditch somewhere, the less drinkable it would be, I set out with empty tin in hand.

I went out the back first, thinking of the rudimentary shower and wondering if there was some sort of other water collection device set up by the previous inhabitants for drinking. I couldn't see anything. I walked along the backs of the other houses in the row, but there was nothing there either.

Having found a bed in the big house, that cluster of buildings seemed like a good place to look for a receptacle of some kind, so back I went. Searching in the kitchen of the big house I found some useful items and noted them mentally for later, but nothing fitting the bill. I looked out the window into the garden area out back. It was a mess with weeds and overgrown bushes growing in haphazard fashion all over the place. But, my eye caught a glimpse of something metallic under a bush near the left-hand wall.

I went to the back door for a closer look. It was made up of several glass panes from top to bottom, held in place by a metal frame covered with peeling white paint and gave a good view of the garden. With this better view I could see an old trailer parked flush against the back of the house. It had wheels, but was perched up on either end with bricks. The tires hung dead flat from the rusted metal of the wheels and the whole thing looked rusted beyond repair. But it wasn't the trailer itself that I was interested in. It was what might be in it.

I opened the back door and went over. Sure enough, there were a couple of rusty old shovels and an old but reasonably serviceable metal bucket inside. It was filled to overflowing with murky water and debris, but so was the trailer, albeit most of the water had dripped through the rotting wood onto the ground beneath. The trailer seemed to be in the perfect place to catch the rainwater running off the room of the house.

I tilted the bucket and poured the grimy water into the trailer. Then I carried it back down to the sea to wash it out. *It might work,* I thought. *Worth a try.*

Back on the shore for the first time since I'd arrived, I stood staring out into the grey nothingness of the horizon. The tide was coming in and each wave smashed and crawled higher up the shore, as if the sea meant to claw its way to me and drag me back into its depths.

Keeping busy had helped to distract me on my first day on the island. But night would come soon. And it is always harder to keep your mind at bay in the dark.

13

The sound of the sea was amplified by the impenetrable darkness. It roared and hissed from all sides, terrorising the island with wave after wave in a never ending siege. I lay wide awake on my bed of old metal, older wood and camping supplies, listening to the assault. I tossed and turned, each time sending the bed frame into a rapture of screeches and grates to join the violent chorus of the sea. I thought I had known the night before. But this was nothing like night-time in the city.

I had sat at my table in the evening and watched the sun go down behind its blanket of cloud, the sky darkening quickly behind it. Before it became too dark to see, I lit my first candle, planting it in the middle of the table. Then I lit another. And another. The candles were precious, but each one gave such little defense against the dark. And I needed light on that first night on the island.

Over the last 24 hours I had crashed from crisis to crisis and I was physically and mentally exhausted. But tired as I was, sleep seemed unlikely. My heart rate was elevated even as I did nothing but sit in the darkness staring at the small flames of the candles one by one. My body wanted to lie down and rest, but my mind resisted. To lay down would be to accept what had happened. To open myself to begin accepting the new normal.

Finally though, as the candles melted down to stubs and unwilling to light more from my limited supply, I blew them out and felt my way through the pitch black house to my makeshift bed.

That first night on the island was the most restless and frightful one of my life. I was tired and did eventually fall asleep, but only for short, sporadic bursts. I was awoken constantly by the unfamiliar noises of the island and the wind which rattled the windows. In my fitful sleep, I had visions of fiery explosions and cold, dark water.

For much of the night I lay awake staring into the abyss around me. When the first hours of daylight dawned, relief washed over me and I drifted off again, finally managing a couple of hours of deep slumber.

When I woke again it was mid-morning and the sun was shining hard through the window of my small cell. I felt wretched, aching all-over and my eyes felt as though they were laden with sand. I got upright and sat on the edge of the bed. It was the first I'd seen of the sun in a good week and the brightness of it stung me.

I rose on unsteady feet and hobbled into the front room. Everything was as I'd left it the night before, my bags strewn about and one chair set apart from the table, where the burnt stubs of the candles sat in hardened pools of wax.

I retrieved my camping stove and fired it up to boil some water. The rush of the gas from the canister felt too fast. The sound of my small supply being burnt away at a frightening pace. *I will need to find fuel for fire,* I thought. Another priority on my growing list.

As the water boiled I couldn't prevent the thoughts and questions of what had happened to the world from entering my mind. I so desperately wanted to know and yet at the same time, to find out would bring with it an awful confirmation of all my fears. Another acceptance that there was no going back.

Sitting at the table I tossed this battle of desire for knowledge versus fear of it, over and over in my head. I had the means to answer my questions. But did I want to? Was I ready?

The coffee helped to stir my senses and the warmth of the sunlight soothed away some of my aches and pains. I decided I would find out later. A few more hours wouldn't change anything after all. A few more days wouldn't either. What had happened, had happened. And there was nothing I could do to change it from this rock in the North Atlantic.

I opened a can of 'Big Breakfast' and ate it cold, unwilling to burn any more gas. The 'Big Breakfast' was mostly baked beans, with the odd piece of egg and miniature sausages which tasted like creamy sawdust here and there. It was not the most inspiring of meals, but it did the trick and coupled with the coffee, I felt human again.

Exploring the island was the priority for today. It was a beautiful sunny morning which showed little sign of rain, so I would have to make the most of it.

I slunk my boots on, still damp from the day before, and went outside to survey my surroundings. I reasoned that the best view of the island would be from top, where I hoped any well or water tower would be easy to spot. But first I would check the other two large buildings I'd spotted from the garden of the big house, just in case there was anything useful in there.

I headed up the track, checking the trailer enroute. I'd returned the bucket to its place, hoping to catch some water, but there hadn't been any rain last night and it was empty. As I approached the end of the village where the two buildings stood, I noticed a large circle of asphalt beside them. There was a faded, barely perceptible "H" painted in the middle. *This must be the famous 'airport',* I thought. And sure enough, on the side of the stone building I recognised the sign I had seen in the pictures online: "Airport Lounge". I guessed this helipad had been the previous inhabitants' lifeline for supplies. There would be no such lifeline for me.

As I had noticed from the big house, the 'Airport Lounge' looked more like a barn. It had high stone walls, a prefabricated metal roof and a large opening at the front. There was a large gate held open by a heavy rock, but its hinges looked rusted and broken and I doubted they would hold at all if I tried to move it.

There was nothing inside the barn, save for

more dirt and dust. Back outside I noticed that there was a smaller building hidden off to the side of it, no bigger than a single room. The door was locked and remembering my accident from the day before, I decided to come back to it once I'd found some kind of tool to pry it open.

The plastic dome on the other side of the barn was a curious structure. It was more like three quarters of a dome with a flat side where the entrance was. It seemed to be in good shape given its age, but perhaps it wasn't as old as the other buildings. I'd had ideas about this building, which could prove crucial to my survival. I ventured inside and felt my boots sink into a springy earth, which stretched out over the considerable expanse of the interior. There was a rusty old pitchfork strewn on the near side and various weeds grew in haphazard bushes all about. It was as I'd suspected. *A greenhouse. The villagers must have grown crops here.*

This was both a relief and revelation. I had assumed that some hardier crops like potatoes, would grow on the island but thought that the potential for more nutritious (not to mention appetising) food like tomatoes would be limited by the harsh climate. The huge greenhouse was a game-changer - it meant that I had a serious chance of cultivating many of the various seeds I'd brought with me into a sustainable food source.

Feeling brighter and very grateful to the previous inhabitants, I struck out from the village for the first time. There was an overgrown dirt track heading upwards from the buildings and curving away to the far side of the hill so I followed it.

The track branched away from the steepest part of the hill, but it was still a tough climb and I was at a loss as to where it would take me. It seemed to be going somewhere, but I couldn't see any more buildings above me and the track seemed to be headed towards the right hand side of the island, which as far as I could tell ended in sharp cliffs. *So why go to the trouble of clearing the path?* I wondered.

As it continued away from the hill, the track levelled out, still going upwards but at a much smaller gradient. I stopped to look back towards the shore and was staggered by how small and far away the buildings looked from up here. I had only been walking for twenty minutes or so and yet the village looked miles away. I stared out at the vast ocean and caught my breath. The feeling of isolation was overwhelming.

Back in London, for the most part I had been living a normal city life. I was a single thirty-something, living in a rented apartment near a busy railroad line, with a mind-numbing middle-management job in IT Security. I went to the gym on Mondays, Tuesdays and Thursdays. On Sundays I went for long runs in the park nearby. Unlike many others, I was the only child from parents who had passed away and I avoided building close relationships. So I felt lonely from time to time, but don't we all? It's easy to be alone in a city of millions.

Being here on this island brought a whole new meaning to the word *alone* though. I had never felt quite so far away from everything. And everyone. It was daunting and depressing.

I pushed on quickly, keen to avoid those thoughts again. Approaching what felt like the middle of the island, the track turned inwards sharply and rose for a few metres or so. And as I crested the rise, my jaw dropped.

14

I stood at the edge of a vast crater, fully 10 metres at its diameter. It was two thirds full with clear water, albeit with a greenish tinge. Being quite some way above the shore, it was all but invisible from the village. This was it. This was how the inhabitants collected their water - a reservoir. *But why build it all the way up here in such an inaccessible place?*

I scanned my eyes over the geography of the island and realised that it made perfect sense. On one side the hill rose steeply upwards to a point and to the other, although it levelled out, the land still rose and ended at cliffs at the back of the island. The crater had been dug in precisely the place where it would capture the most rainwater both from the sky and running off from the higher ground above it. It was simple, yet brilliant.

I thought again of those old inhabitants who had abandoned this place long ago. My admiration for them soared. It had gotten too much for them in the end and they had been forced to leave, but my god they had given it a good shot. I said another silent thank you to the people whose efforts in the past had given me the chance of a future.

It occurred to me that it was going to take an awful lot of trips up here to keep myself stocked with water back at the house. I made a mental note to try and think of a better plan for that, but since I was up there I decided to continue exploring.

I was still shattered from the previous day and the highest point of the island seemed too much, so I continued in the opposite direction, towards the cliffs. The track had ended at the lip of the reservoir and the ground underfoot was lumpy, covered with grass and interspersed with sharp rocks. I trod carefully, all too aware of what a twisted ankle or broken arm would mean. It was slow going but I pressed on to the top of the island.

I was so focused on picking my steps that I failed to notice the edge of the island approaching and nearly went right over the cliff. Taking a few steps back I gaped at the unsettling site. The jagged cliff edge dropped straight down two hundred feet to the ocean below. Where the edge of the island met the angry sea at the bottom, it was strewn with rocks pointed like daggers back up towards me. It felt like I was standing at the very edge of the world.

I was about to turn back when I noticed an odd white substance all along the edge of the cliffs. It didn't seem natural like a limescale or moss coating, but it was everywhere. Reaching down I scratched some off and rubbed it between my fingers. *Bird shit.*

Mounds and mounds of the white and grey

excrement lined the cliff edge. Rubbing my hand hard against my thigh in disgust, I looked around and listened. I thought I could make out the squawking of birds over the roar of the waves crashing around below me. And then I saw them, swooping and gliding to and from the cliffs below me. There were hundreds of them, big and small and of varying colours, white and black, brown and grey.

I stood and watched them for quite some time. It was a fascinating site and being there with them eased my isolation.

Best of all, it gave me an idea. Something to consider in the future anyway.

15

As I made my way back down to the village it struck me that I hadn't seen a single tree on the island. I had hoped to scavenge wood for fire and repairs to the roof. But the tallest plants on the island were no more than bushes.

There was some old wood scattered about in the village and a bit of driftwood on the shore, but this would run out very quickly. It was warm enough despite the seemingly permanent cool breeze on the island, but it was June - I shuddered to think what it would be like in winter. This felt like a major issue. The only thing I could think of for the time being was to scavenge as much driftwood as I could.

I was tired from the hike but I went all the way down to the shore line anyway, to collect what I could. There were bits and pieces here and there, but no meaningful amount. I decided to store what I could find now and dry it out in case of an emergency.

I went over to the dock. *Plenty of wood here,* I

thought. Dismantling the dock would also make it harder and less welcoming for any other people to get to the island. Not that I expected anyone to try.

It was still a beautiful day and the sun warmed both my muscles and my soul. For the first time since I came up with the idea, I had a genuine feeling that it might just work out. I had water, enough food to last me for a while and an adequate shelter. What I didn't have though, was any information about what had happened since I left. I couldn't put it off any longer. I had to know.

I headed back to the house and assembled the pile of wood by the fireplace. *I should unpack first,* I thought, my mind doing that clever trick that our brains do, of finding other priorities when there's something important that we don't really want to do.

I got all of the tins and other foodstuffs out first and stored them in the kitchen cupboards. I left three of them to one side; these would go into a backpack with some other essentials - a flight bag, just in case.

Next was the can opener, a small hunting knife and other cutlery, which also went into the kitchen with the camping stove, matches, two lighters and the candles. I organised the fishing equipment I'd brought along the wall in a corner of the living room. After that came my clothing, which I placed in neat piles in the bedroom, and one last item in the large hold-all which I hoped never to have to use. I stashed it under the bed for safe-keeping.

I looked around me. Just the cool-box left.

I sat at the table, undid the lock and pried the lid off carefully. Inside I'd stashed the things that it was most important to keep dry. The cool-box was airtight and unlike the other bags, if it had spilled overboard enroute to the island, it would have floated. In theory at least. I pulled the contents out one by one: There were the packs of seeds for various crops, some water purification tablets, a leather-bound notebook with three biros and there at the bottom, inside a plastic bag and wrapped in a towel, was a wind-up radio.

I unwrapped it and sat with it in my hands, looking it over. It was a simple red box with a tuning dial, aerial, volume knob and single speaker. On the top was a solar panel and at the back was a large black hand crank, both of which could be used to charge it up. The radio was waterproof, but I hadn't taken any chances.

I remembered packing it, wrapping it in the towel to prevent it being banged about on the journey and sealing it in the container. It was to be my lifeline to the outside world and a symbol of hope. In my denial I had reasoned that I would go to the island as a precautionary measure, wait until the news got better and then return. But now, sitting here on this island and knowing that nuclear war had begun, that felt like a desperate delusion.

I cranked the handle for longer than I probably needed to. I just kept going until each of my arms in turn begged for rest. Then I put the radio on the table in front of me and extended the aerial. I hesitated for a moment longer and then finally switched it on.

At first there was nothing but static, loud and haunting over the sound of the sea, but after some tuning I found a station. It was faint, with a lot of distortion but I could make it out well enough.

The news was not good. The broadcaster was stern but breathless, pitching between updates and repeating the main report over and over.

"...widespread devastation. Many of the world's major cities have been reduced to flaming rubble. Clouds of radioactive particles cover much of what remains. The death-toll is uncountable but is thought to be in the hundreds of millions. We are not able to provide you with government advice at this time, but scientists we have spoken to advise anyone remaining to get as far away from strike points as they can, seeking cover underground if possible."

The bombs in Britain had not been the only ones. In a pre-emptive strike, Russia had launched missiles at several major U.S. cities and European cities. The U.S. had responded the moment they detected the initial missile launches, launching missiles of its own on Moscow and St Petersburg, as well as at China and North Korea.

Common sense had given way to paranoia. One attack had led to another and another. Half the major cities of the world had been obliterated. It was World War Three. The final war. The last war of humanity, where our technology and our fear of each other finally destroyed us.

I sat with my head in my hands, sucking in air

in great gasps. A tidal wave of despondency crashed over me. Without warning, my chest heaved and the tears came spilling down my cheeks and onto the dusty floor. The panic and emotion I'd held back over the last few days all came out in guttering sobs.

I was in a state of disbelief. Even though I'd seen this coming, planned and executed an escape and heard when London was struck, I still couldn't believe it had come to this. How had we let this happen? For make no mistake, there was no one blameless here. We had ignored the struggles of the common man. We had allowed politicians to feed on our fears. We had stood by while they stoked the volcano to eruption.

I sat like that for several hours, periodically crying and shivering until my body had no more to give and I lay my head on the table, exhausted.

There were reports of looting, the first sign of societal breakdown, and of widespread panic. Law enforcement was non-existent, hit by mass loss of life and the failure of many officers to show up. And who could blame them? Work no longer mattered when the world was being destroyed.

I sat there for hours listening to it all from my seat at the edge of the world. Devastated and disbelieving, frozen and frightened, guilty that I had somehow survived. But for how long?

Unable to take any more I switched the radio off. Outside, the sun had disappeared and dusk menaced the sky. It would soon be night again.

16

After another restless night, punctuated with dreams of destruction and panic, I awoke to an overcast and windswept day. A weariness had settled inside me, so deep that I could feel it in my bones. I lay on my back for some time staring at the ceiling, despondent.

I tried to steel myself. It came down to a simple choice: I could get busy surviving - do everything I could to make a go of it, or I could succumb to depression - eat my way through my supplies and drown myself in the sea.

I thought that even if I wanted to end it, I probably wouldn't have the courage to. I would end up trying to survive at the last minute, failing and then dying slowly from starvation. No, if that was going to happen, I may as well start trying right away and give myself a better chance. Go down fighting. Plus, the busier I was, the better I would feel.

Stages.

I rose suddenly, buoyed by the thought that I

owed it not just to myself, but to the people I had come to know throughout my life. The people I'd grown up with. The people I'd conversed and worked with. The people that never stood a chance when the bomb dropped. I would survive for them all.

Drinking my morning coffee, I tried to prioritise what needed to be done. Crops would take time to grow, the sooner I planted them the better. That was the first task for today. The sooner I could catch fish or find another food source, the longer my supplies would last, so that would come next. I still needed to search the rest of the buildings and figure out a better way to transport water down from the reservoir, but those things could wait for now.

I had printed copious notes from the internet, on how to plant and tend to various crops. I read them through at the table while I ate half a can of corned beef. I would plant everything except a few potatoes in the plastic dome. If they all grew I would have a wealth of vegetables and a few fruits. Then I could take some of the hardy looking plants and try to grow them out the back of my house for convenience. The few potatoes leftover I would try out back right away, as I figured they were the most likely to grow outside.

Although it was a cloudy and cool day, inside the dome it got warmer as the day went on. By mid-morning I had shed both my hoodie and my t-shirt. I hadn't brought any big tools with me as they would be heavy and unwieldy. I'd brought a trowel and mini fork would probably do. This was a mistake. The old pitchfork I'd found was useful but without a decent shovel most of the work had to be done on my hands and knees. It was hard back-breaking work which took me all morning and into the early afternoon, just to clear half the ground, prepare the soil and plant some seeds. I could see I would be spending a lot of time in the dome.

But I was pleased with my work though. Everything was planted in neat rows, with spaces between to walk through and water them. To allow rain in, one side of the roof of the dome could be slid open via a stiff lever near the door, but there was no rain today. So I made several begrudging trips up the reservoir and back with the bucket, conscious again that I needed to find a better way to get water down into the village.

After a short break to finish the corned beef from the morning and rest my aching back, I headed back up the island. I wanted to scale the hill and survey my surroundings from the highest point on the island. This would give me sight of anything I had missed so far and a better general view of the lay of the land, in case for any reason, I needed to hide somewhere on the island.

Climbing the hill was agony after my morning of grafting in the soil. It started steep and only got steeper and the terrain was uneven and difficult to traverse. To get to the narrow, flat point at the top, I had to jump and pull myself up over the rocky side. The effort was worth it though. The island looked spectacular from its highest point, so green and beautiful in a contrast to the deep blue sea surrounding it. The wind was stronger up there and I sat down to take it all in, for fear of being blown off.

The hilltop itself was at the very rear of the island and off to one side. To its front was the rest of the island but behind it fell away at a sharp angle all the way down to the sea. The steep hillside was like a green backdrop to the stage of the village, with its greys and browns. All around it was punctuated at random intervals by large boulders which were dotted about and seemed to balance on the hillside with perfect grace.

The cliffs I'd been to were on the other side, but they began here and stretched right the way around the back of the island. It was as if it were once a part of a bigger land mass and had been cleaved in two, the other half swallowed up by the ocean. It was a dramatic landscape, made even more so by the fact there was nothing else to be seen but the sea on every horizon.

Besides a stone walled area a short distance from the dome, there weren't any more buildings that I could see. The reservoir was clear from up there but there weren't any other man made features that I could make out. There was however, a wide ledge a couple of metres across, which seemed to start at a narrow point on the cliffs near the hilltop and disappear from view below the back of the island.

The ledge was rammed with all different types of birds. It was difficult to tell from so high up, but I thought I could see the tell-tale coloured beaks of a few puffins. The ledge narrowed out as it fell behind the cliffs but it did seem to form a natural, albeit dangerous looking path down. I decided to head down for a closer look, my initial ideas about the birds coming back to me.

At the top of the cliff there wasn't really a path at all, just a few loose rocks. The wind whipped my hair around, as if to warn me away, but my curiosity overcame any trepidation I felt. A bit further down the path looked more solid, so I sat on the edge and lowered myself carefully down, testing the stability of the rocks with a bit of my weight at a time. Once fully down, there was barely enough room for my feet to stand side by side and I grasped the side of the cliff with white knuckles. I could feel the drop from the ledge to the sea behind me and my legs felt suddenly very weak. But I could hear the birds now and I wanted to get closer.

Gradually, I inched my way down until the ledge opened up to a more comfortable width. Still holding on to the jagged rocks wherever I could, I made my way around to the nesting spot. The din here was remarkable. The birds were either tussling for position, diving into the depths or sitting watching me. My approach didn't seem to trouble them at all. I reasoned that this was because they hadn't had much contact with humans.

I got to within half a metre of them and sat down. There were puffins, cormorants and gannets among others that I didn't recognise. I watched for a while, fascinated by my new friends. A brave white cormorant sauntered over to me for a closer look. Once he'd done evaluating me, a few others came over. It seemed that I was quite the curiosity.

The puffins kept their distance on the far side of the ledge and were also dotted all along the cliff where the rocks stuck out just enough for them to sit. They were the most beautiful bird I had ever seen, their big beaks a kaleidoscope of orange, grey, white and red.

I was broken from my reverie by a cormorant who had made his way right in front of me and squawked at such a volume that I jerked back, sending him flapping back towards the others. I needed to focus. I had come here for a reason.

The very thought of it appalled me. They looked so at ease and defenceless up here, immune to the threat of mankind. I didn't want to hurt them. I didn't even want to disturb them.

I scolded myself. There I was, just another first world coward who was happy to eat meat, so long as it came in plastic packaging and didn't resemble a living creature. Only, things were different now. There wouldn't be any more pre-prepared chicken breasts ready to chop up and toss in the wok. The only food I had was in cans and it wouldn't last forever. A fish or a bird or a potato; they were all living things that I would have to eat to survive.

The softer side of my mind tried to convince me that I could come back another time, work my way up to it. But the harder side, the part of me that had hidden in plain sight for years, escaped an apocalypse and been thrown out to sea in the middle of the night, knew that I had to do this. There were hundreds of birds and only one me. This was the way of things.

If I was going to survive I would have to do this several times over. Better to get the first one out of the way and numb myself to the horror. I closed my eyes and tried to visualise doing the deed.

17

I sat there like that for several minutes, with my eyes closed and the birds squawking all around me. Then I opened my eyes, gritted my teeth and waited for my next opportunity. I didn't have to wait long.

After the initial surprise the birds nearest me had settled again and many were still curious about this new arrival. I fixed my eyes on one of the bigger ones and stayed as still as I could while he ventured around me in an ever decreasing circle, until he was right in front of me. I took a deep breath and grabbed him.

I had intended to break its neck with a quick twist of my wrist, but I was so tightly sprung and the bird so slight, that I took his head clean off in one go. The sudden motion alarmed the birds nearby into flight, which set others off behind them. The instant flurry and sound shocked me and my torso flew backwards, rebounding off the cliff face and onto my side with my shoulder and head hanging out over the cliff. I scrambled back up and sat breathing hard with one hand wrapped around the body of the cormorant and the other I realised, still enclosed around its head. I tossed it over the side and reeled in shock.

I looked down at my quarry, the poor lifeless shape of a small bird. My hands were covered in blood and stained feathers. I felt wretched.

I clambered back up the path, desperate to be away from the scene of the crime and the panic of the flock. I took the bird back to the house in a daze, sickened by what I had done.

Once home, I plucked it and cleaned it up as best I could, determined to see it through so that the poor thing had not been killed for nothing. It took much longer than I thought to get all the little feathers out and it was grim work. By the time I was finished the carcass looked a lot smaller and hardly worth the effort. I chopped it into pieces anyway, removing as many bones as I could and then cooked it up on my camping stove.

I sat at the table with no appetite at all. Despite the physical strain of the day, the heavy feeling of killing the bird had sapped my hunger. But it did smell good and I forced myself to take a tentative bite.

The cormorant tasted both gamey and fishy at the same time. It wasn't unpleasant. In fact, the more I ate of it, the more I liked it. By the end of the small meal my appetite had returned and I was hungry for more.

Not willing to open another can just to fill my stomach, I tried to drown out my hunger by turning on the radio. Once again, the voice of a strained newsreader filled my little cabin. More missiles, more fighting, more civil unrest. The terrible updates bounced off the walls and reverberated in my chest. I could only listen for a short while.

At the bottom of another mental trough, I tried to reflect on my achievements from the day. Seeds planted – check. Hill climbed and island surveyed – check. A meal made from the resources on the island – check. Not too bad for a day's work.

There was still so much to do though. I still wanted to go through the rest of the buildings and I needed to fix the leaking roof. I would have to tend to the plants daily and that meant an awful lot of water runs unless the rain came in. It was important to inventory my food supplies and plan a ration and I wanted to try fishing too. The house also needed cleaning as the dirt and dust were getting to my lungs, particularly at night. The list was endless and just thinking about it made me weary.

As the light started to fade I took to bed. Exhausted both from the effort of the day and the lack of meaningful rest over the last few, I was out to it almost as soon as my head hit the makeshift pillow of my hoodie. I slept for at least three hours before waking to the dreadful darkness again.

18

The next few days were filled with more activity. Much of my time was taken up transporting water down from the reservoir, either to the dome or to my house. I had begun using the cool-box instead of the bucket. This meant I could carry more water each journey with less spills, but it was much heavier and took a lot more effort. I still hadn't been able to come up with a better plan.

I searched the remaining buildings and found yet more items left behind, some of which were very useful. Out the back of the third house I found an old ladder which at first did not inspire confidence, but turned out to be robust enough when I used it to clear out the drain on top of the shower and survey the damage on the roof.

I also found a few empty jars, which would serve well for glasses and some other bits of furniture including a bookcase half filled with dusty books, and a small stool which would make a decent bedside table.

Strangest of all was the small building to the side of the barn. It took several attempts to break the door open with the trowel, but once inside I was surprised at what had been left behind. Unlike the other buildings, everything inside the small room looked untouched. There was a metal table with a single chair and what looked like a world war two communications radio, complete with microphone and headset. The sight of it unsettled me. I didn't touch it for fear of setting it off and alerting anybody to my presence on the island. The news from the mainland had grown steadily worse with reports of uncontrolled nuclear blazes, lawlessness and armed gangs. I felt safe hidden away alone up here and wanted to remain that way.

Over the next few weeks I made several attempts at fishing. At first I tried sitting at the end of the doc and tossing the line out as far as I could. After several hours and nothing to show for it but a tiny sprat, I realised I would have to get further out. My boat had ores strapped to the inside and I used these to row out a ways from the island. I waited for the seas to calm before attempting it, still wary from my trip overboard that first torrid night.

It took a while, trying varying lures and techniques, to get a result. I found that a brightly coloured lure with a good weight, slung out and then slowly dragged back in, worked best. It was touch and go but I caught two herring in half an hour using this method. That was a banner moment indeed and my first happy evening on the island. I ate like a king and still had some leftover for breakfast the next morning.

I could only go out when the sea was calm but I stuck with fishing initially, over catching more birds. After a period of three days of rough weather, when pushing off from shore was not an option, I grit my teeth and went back up in search of the flock. I'd almost hoped they'd moved on but they were still on the ledge where I 'd left them. I had wondered if the shock of my first attack would have made them more cautious of me and difficult to catch. This was not the case however.

The second time around was only a bit less sickening than the first. It was something that would take a long time to get used to.

It rained on and off on the island and I raced up to the dome to open the roof whenever the clouds turned a dark and menacing grey. There wasn't a great deal of activity the first couple of weeks, but before long the first green shoots started emerging. It filled me with relief.

Life on the island was a constant roller coaster of ecstatic highs and troughs of depression. But I settled into a routine, which helped stave off my fears and fight the despondency. In the mornings, I would tend to the plants and make water runs. In the afternoons, I would fish, collect driftwood or carry out repairs.

In the evenings I would eat while listening to the radio. There was never anything other than a rolling newscast filled with ever worsening gloom. At some point I noticed that the usual changing guard of the presenters stopped and for a couple of weeks there was only ever the same male voice on the airwaves. He sounded very young and the news seemed to become less globally focused and more regional.

And then one night, even he was gone. I spent an hour turning the tuning dial from left to right, desperate to find another station. After several turns all the way up and down the band without success I gave up. I spent a restless night imagining the worst. I tried again on successive evenings and at different times during the day. But there was never anything to be found but the angry hiss of white noise.

19

I awoke from a deep slumber with a start, the sound of a bee buzzing around the window piercing my ears. It was a clear, sunny day and by the look of the light, I'd overslept.

The day to day physical activity had been tough, but the benefit I'd gained was a better quality of sleep. I was still having the odd rough night but they were becoming less frequent as time went on.

I lay back with my eyes closed and tried to block out the incessant buzzing. The day before I had collected rocks and fallen bits of the stone wall from the garden, to build a makeshift guard around the fireplace in the living room and provide more space for cooking. My arms and chest were still aching from the effort. I thought the bee must have flown in and got trapped while the back door was open.

Being a remote island, I hadn't really seen many insects at all. I was sure there must be some crawling around in the undergrowth but I hadn't really noticed many. There were flowers up on the hillside so something must be pollinating them, but I hadn't seen any bees either.

The fireplace extension had gone well. I'd used the flatter stones from the wall as the base and then placed the more jagged rocks around it, forming a pit. I used smaller stones to try to fill in any holes left by the bigger rocks. There was ample space in the middle for burning the wood that I'd found. I laid the springy metal frame from an old armchair across the top as a mesh.

I hadn't tried it yet but planned to just as soon as I caught some more herring. The camping stove was nearly empty and this would have to be my long-term solution. So long as I could find enough wood. One problem at a time though.

The buzzing grew louder and angrier. I opened my eyes in case the bee was flying near my head. I had no intention of getting stung. I couldn't see it. I craned my neck at an uncomfortable angle to get a full view of the window. Nothing. How odd.

Then it hit me, harder than a storm wave at high tide. It wasn't the buzzing of a bee that I could hear. It was the sound of a boat engine. And it was getting closer.

END OF PART ONE

PART TWO

1

Getting a gun had been the easy part. I had thought buying a gun in Britain, with its strict gun laws, would be difficult. But simply by typing *Gun* into an online classifieds site, I found a landowner out in the country, who had "just bought a shiny new hunting rifle" and didn't "need the old-boy anymore". "Still shoots just fine" he'd put. One phone call later and I'd arranged to pick it up on my way up to Scotland.

Buying the gun heightened my paranoia as I fled London. Not because I hadn't used one before or that it was illegal without a license, but because it brought to mind the reasons why I was buying one in the first place. Like everyone, I'd seen post-apocalyptic movies and TV shows. I believed that humanity was essentially good, but in desperate and lawless times, anything could happen. Hiding a gun in my car made me uncomfortable, even if it was just for defence.

'You have all the necessary I suppose?' he'd asked me, referring to a licence.

'Oh yes,' I said, pretending to look-over and admire the rifle. I didn't offer to show him and he didn't ask. But I'd printed off a decent forgery just in case.

I planned my route north to take in camping shops that meant the least deviation from the M1 motorway, which led all the way up from London to Newcastle. I had to visit several to make sure I could get everything I needed. And I was conscious never to buy too much in one place and prompt any friendly conversation about what kind of trip I was planning.

By the time I got to Scotland I had everything I needed except a boat and the fuel I would need to run it. At a gas station on the border I tried to buy two jerry cans, but the attendant refused.

'Can't sell you two mate. Only one, that's the law.'

'Ah,' I said, trying to act natural and already anticipating his next question. 'No problem, one should be fine.'

'Why'd you need two anyway?'

'My grandmother lives in the highlands. No mains power, only a generator. Her usual supplier has… stuffed up again.'

'Ah right. Pain in the neck those guys. My uncle used to live out there too and they were always letting him down. They just don't get how important it is. Mind you, they're all staffed by immigrants these days. No idea. Anyway, just the one then?'

I nodded as if I understood exactly what he meant. Then I filled the can, paid for the fuel in cash, drove down the road to the next gas station and bought another.

The boat was next. But I didn't know where to start. There aren't many shops selling cheap second hand boats. The online classifieds were no good either. The boats were either too expensive or too far away. Part of the problem was that I was trying to buy one in a remote part of Scotland nearby where I intended to launch from. The other part was that I needed to buy it on or near the water. I couldn't afford a trailer to tow it anywhere. It had to be ready to go. I could hardly wonder about town asking random people if they had a boat to sell either.

I took to driving around the marinas in the small towns that dotted the coast looking for any 'for sale' signs. There were none. After several hours of searching and running out of time, I decided to try a scrap merchant on the outskirts of a fishing village. The man running it was dressed in a greasy orange boilersuit that was almost as ancient as he was. He had an accent so thick I could barely understand him.

'Cannae tak' ony o' thae boats oot oan th` sea! Ahr ye mad?' he was shaking his head so hard I thought it might fall off his bony neck.

'I see,' I said, hoping I'd understood him correctly - the boats he had weren't seaworthy. 'I was hoping to get a cheap one. But it needs to float of course. Typical English landlubber' I smiled in an attempt to build a bit of rapport.

'Ye cannae, ye cannae' he repeated and made to walk away. Then he stopped suddenly and spun back.

'How larige a boat dae ye need?

'Well... big enough to go hopping round the coast.' That seemed reasonable, without giving away anything.

'Ian mae hae something for ye. Hing oan a wee sec.'

He disappeared into his shack. Ten minutes later he came back with a dirty scrap of paper and handed it to me. There were lines and arrows scrawled all over it and after a moment I discerned it was a map.

'Gang see Ian. He'll sort ye oot.'

I thanked the man and returned to my car, where I sat for some time trying to work the map out.

After a few wrong turns and backtracks, I found my way to another small coastal village. The building the map seemed to indicate was a pub, rather than a house. I went inside and asked the barman if he knew an Ian. As luck would have it, it was him.

The old fellow had called ahead and told him about me. He walked me down to the small port and showed me the dinghy. By this point I was so desperate I would have bought a rubber raft if that was what he was selling. But the dinghy looked solid and reliable enough and the price was right. I handed over the cash then and there and he left me to it.

I piloted the boat out of the port and around the coast to the remote bay, where I beached it, clambered up the cliff and set off on foot to retrieve the car. Night had fallen by the time I got back. It was supposed to be my last ever night on the mainland. But I didn't count on meeting the others.

2

In the back of my mind I feared this day might come. But from everything I'd heard on the radio it had seemed less and less likely as time went by. I had come too far to lose St. Rita now. This was my island, my salvation, and I intended to protect it.

The sound of the boat fired me into a panic. I jumped out of my makeshift bed and tore my clothes on, growling in frustration when my foot got caught in the leg of my jeans and slowed me down. The sound of the boat grew ever louder. I thrust my hand under the bed and grasped cold metal.

I tore out the door with the rifle in my hand. *Just in case,* I thought. *Just in case.*

For all I knew, the boat wasn't coming to the island at all. There were dozens of little islands to the North of Scotland and it could be headed to any one of them. The boat could be filled with good people just trying to survive like me. But I had no way of knowing. What I knew for sure though, was that I wouldn't give up my survival without a fight. If anyone tried to steal my supplies or evict me from the island, they would have to do so by force.

The thought of firing the gun at someone terrified me. But I hoped that simply the sight of it would give anyone with bad intentions a second thought. And if I had to use it, I would.

I raced down to the shore, breath heavy and heart pounding in my ears. I reached the beach just as the boat was docking next to the old wooden port.

The boat surprised me. I'd pictured an old sea faring vessel or an oil covered tug boat. But the boat pulling in was more like a medium-sized pleasure cruiser. It was all white, with chrome banisters from bow to stern and beige lounger cushions on the front.

From where I stood at the shore-end of the dock, I couldn't make out any people, but I could see that the boat tugged a large trailer behind it, loaded with several big blue barrels and wooden crates.

The engine was killed and a short, heavy-set man hopped out. He was focused on tying the boat to the dock and had the back of his balding to me.

'Stop!' I shouted, in as firm a voice as I could muster.

The man jumped and another rope, thrown to him from inside the boat, hit him in the chest. He staggered backwards and raised his hands to chest level. We were 30 metres apart and so far as I could see, he wasn't carrying a weapon. I was keen to push the advantage of surprise.

'This island is taken. Move on. Now.'

The man was frozen to the spot, eyes going from me to the gun and back again. My glare was fixed on him, but I saw the face of a woman with light brown hair poke around the side of the boat from above him.

I felt an easing in my chest and railed against it. If this was a married man, or even better a family man, then perhaps he was less of a threat. But I couldn't make those assumptions. No matter what, I had to be fully alert. Ready to shoot.

I considered firing a shot into the sky. But by the look on the man's face, the sight of the gun had already had the desired effect.

'Sir…' he began

'What are you waiting for? Get back on your boat and get the hell away from my island!' I still didn't know if I could bring myself to shoot but for all I knew, his polite approach could just be an act.

'We mean you know harm' he said, hands still raised.

'I don't care what you *mean*. Didn't you hear me? This island is taken, now get out of here!'

The woman on the boat came out with her hands up, stepping gingerly onto the dock.

'Please don't shoot. We're no threat to you'

Her voice was shaking. Guilt rose up from my stomach. I had scared her and was behaving like a monster. *Focus. No risks. Nothing is worth the island.*

She noticed me hesitate and seized upon it..

'Are you alone here?'

'Yes' I said and immediately regretted it. *Stupid,* I thought. *Very stupid. There could be more of them on the boat.*

'Sir…' the man began again. But before he could continue another man was climbing over the side, hands raised. Before I could shout out again I caught a glimpse of another woman on the boat, pulling two children back from behind one of the windows. There was a flash of blond and she was gone.

'How many are you on that boat?' I demanded.

'Five,' said the new man. He was taller and slimmer than the other, with short grey hair that he looked to be cutting himself. He had a look of grim determination on his face and didn't seem as anxious as the others. Both men were middle to late-middle age, as was the woman. 'Well..' he continued, 'Five adults and two children'.

Seven people. Well five and a half anyway. Against just me. But I had the only gun, as far as I could tell.

'This is not a negotiation. You have thirty seconds to get back aboard and ship out.' My voice sounded harsh and angry. This wasn't me, I wasn't a monster. But I'd heard the radio reports. This was the world now. I must *act* the monster to survive.

'Please,' the woman said again, 'We're not here to hurt or steal from you. We're just trying to escape. We've come a long way and the children are tired. What's happening on the mainland is…'

Tears filled her eyes and she began to weep. The shorter man put an arm round her and drew her to his chest, but kept his other hand raised.

The taller man took a step towards me. 'Sir…'

I fired a shot into the air.

'Stay where you are!' He stepped back again, his grimace replaced with a look of alarm. But he continued talking.

'Sir, we can help you. If you're on your own here, we can help. We have fuel,' he indicated toward the trailer at the back of the boat. 'We have a generator. *Power…*' his voice tailed off. I could sense his desperation.

Then a third woman appeared on the side of the boat. I remained focused on the taller man on the dock, but out of the corner of my eye I could see she had one hand gripped to the banister for balance, the other raised in supplication.

'Stay there!' I shouted, without looking at her. I could feel myself losing the advantage. The longer I went without getting rid of or shooting at them, the safer they would feel. I could get off only two more shots before I had to reload. Would I have enough time if they rushed me?

This was not how I had envisioned this scenario. In my imagination, my gruff voice and appearance, coupled with the rifle, had always been enough to move any threat on. I had tried not to think about the next step. The one where they leave but come back with their own guns and reinforcements, in the middle of the night.

'If you'll let me…' the woman from the boat started. She swallowed a gulp before continuing 'I just wanted to say, we understand.' This caught me off guard. I looked up at her and was startled.

She was younger than the other three and her beauty was striking. Bright blue eyes stood out against a pale complexion and long brown hair framed her face in waves. My lack of immediate response emboldened her to go on.

'Are you a refugee like us?' she asked. I nodded. I hadn't thought of myself like that. But that's what I was. I returned my eyes to the three on the dock. Their eyes were trained on me, but they hadn't moved.

'Then we know what you're going through. We're trying to escape too. Some people have become animals. But we're not animals. We're just… we thought we might find safety out here.' From the rear of the boat I heard the muffled cries of children being hushed by their mother.

I wanted to say I didn't care. I wanted to fire into the sky and drive them away. For all their supposed innocence, I knew they could pose a very serious threat to me. But in the face of such anguish I was stalling. And my hesitation gave them hope.

'What's your name sir?' the young woman on the boat asked.

My name.

'Carl.' I said. It sounded false even to my own ears. But the strangers didn't seem to notice.

'Carl.' She repeated. 'I'm Maisie.' She cast a

nervous waive with one of her upright hands.

We stood for a moment in silence, looking at each other.

'I'm Jake' said the tall man, his voice uncertain, 'and this…is Steve and his wife Susan.'

Susan tried to smile but it was weak and she was clearly terrified. She clung onto her husband. Jake continued

'On the boat are my wife Karen and our two children. Tom and Aileen.'

'Carl,' said Maisie, 'We're good people. We're good people Carl and we mean you no harm. I'm sure there's lots of room on this island. If you could just trust us…'

Trust, I thought. *The most important thing of all. The greatest or most fool-hardy thing a person can do.*

I had forgotten what it was like to trust. It went further back for me then my arrival on the island. Or even in London. I had lived a quiet but purposeful existence, keeping friendships at bay. Never allowing anyone to get too close. Because that was the way it had to be.

Society had fallen and I had come here to survive. By myself. But what was the point in surviving alone? By default, I hadn't ever really considered that. I just wanted to live. I didn't want to die in a nuclear war, or suffer some other horrendous fate at the hands of others. I'd been running on instinct. But I hadn't considered what came after that. I hadn't considered what it would all be for in the long run. For the first time I asked myself what the difference was between dying when the first bomb hit, or dying twenty years later, alone on a godforsaken rock?

Fear is the enemy of trust. It builds walls, creates divides and perpetuates paranoia. But it's also easy. There's no risk in fear. Trust however, takes bravery.

I had thought of myself as brave. A fearless survivor who fought the world and struggled on. But my escape was not born of bravery, it was born out of fear. Everything I'd done to get to this point had been because of fear. Fear of death, fear of others, fear of the unknown. I wasn't as strong as I thought I was. I was a coward. A coward pointing a gun at a scared and desperate family.

I realised in that moment that I was tired of being afraid. I took the bravest decision I would ever take in my life and lowered the rifle.

Relief washed over their faces. But trust takes time.

'There are rules,' I said.

3

‘First,’ I said, ‘No one is to come within six feet of me’.

I would keep the rifle with me at all times. If any of them got too close, I would warn them off. If they tried anything, I would shoot. At least, I hoped I would.

‘Second, my house is the second one of the row of terraced buildings. You do not approach it and you never venture inside. You can have any other building you like, but that one is mine. Is that understood?’

They nodded, still in shock but grateful not to have a gun pointed at them.

‘Finally,’ I said, ‘I will share what I have, but you must share what you’ve brought’.

‘Thank you, Carl’ said Maisie. She stepped off the boat. ‘We know what a leap of faith this is for you and we will do whatever we need to earn your trust.’

‘That’s right’ said the heavy-set man.

'Whatever it takes'. He was nodding hard.

Their eagerness to adapt to my precautions put me at ease. There were no arguments. They hadn't expected anyone to be here and were relieved that I hadn't shot them or tried to steal from them. On the surface at least, it really did seem like they just wanted to live.

We stood looking at each other for a while longer, until I realised they were waiting for me to direct their next steps.

'Ok,' I said. 'Grab what you need and I'll give you a quick tour of the island. We can unload the rest of the stuff later.'

I watched them carefully, making sure they didn't carry a knife or any other weapon off the boat. The remaining passengers, Karen and her two children, were helped out onto the dock and Jake tested the moorings. The only thing they brought with them were a couple of bottles of water. The children, a boy and a girl between 10 and 12 had tired faces and their eyes were red where they had been crying. A wave of guilt washed over me.

Once they were all offloaded, they made their way slowly down the dock towards me. I tightened my grip around the shotgun.

'Six feet, remember'. They nodded.

I had them walk in front of me as I directed them up towards the village. Although the gun was slung over my shoulder, I remained on high alert. At any minute, I expected one of them to turn and make a lunge for me. I had resolved to try to hit them with the butt of the gun if they did. Firing would be a last resort.

The two children frequently glanced back at me and the gun, their big eyes shining with fear. Their mother did her best to stop them staring, giving them stern looks and pats on the back. I had no interest in frightening children, but for now at least, this was how it had to be.

I guided them up past the small row of houses and into the square, indicating my new home as we went and reiterating that it was off limits. I pointed out the big house and suggested they may want to set up there initially. Partly because they appeared to be an extended family and partly because it was far enough from my home that I might hear them coming.

None of them spoke much more than a word. Instead they gave furtive nods of approval at my suggestions.

We continued on and up to the dome. On the way I told them about the various crops I had planted inside and the mechanism to open the roof. They seemed both impressed and more relaxed at this. Even more so once they had had a look inside.

'That's a lot of work you've put in' offered Jake.

'It was,' I agreed. 'But it helped. You know… keeping busy.'

He nodded.

'What's in there?' the young boy asked, pointing to the small building off to the side of the barn. His mother went to shush him with a look of panic.

'It's ok,' I said. 'I think it was a small office of sorts. There's nothing in there now.'

It was a lie but an important one. The radio would need to remain a secret until I learned whether these people truly were refugees. And alone. My secret isle needed to remain that way.

Our secret isle. It would take a while to adjust to the thought.

I was living moment to moment, as I'm sure they were. I still thought of them as dangerous intruders in my home. But deep down I hoped it would work out. It would be nice to have some help around the island.

I explained the water situation and gave directions to the reservoir, but suggested the rest of the tour wait until they had brought their goods on shore and had a rest. They agreed with relief.

We walked in silence back down to the beach. We were all of us, on the very edge of our nerves.

'So… we'll unload and take everything up to the big house?' Steve asked.

'Yes' I said. 'I'll help you. It looks like you have quite a bit of stuff'

'Thank you' said Jake. I wasn't sure he meant it. He wasn't any more over his suspicion of me than I was of them. 'We do. We came well prepared'.

More so than me, I thought. *But they had more time and a bigger boat.*

'How will this umm… work?' asked Jake. It

took me a second to understand what he meant. He was conscious of my six feet rule. I thought for a moment.

'We'll form a chain. You and your wife unload the boat and I'll carry everything to the end of the dock. The rest of you can take it from there, up to the house.'

'The barrels are very heavy,' Steve said. 'They'll be a two-man job'.

I nodded.

'Ok, leave anything really heavy until last. Then we'll work something out'.

Jake wasn't lying when he'd said they'd come well prepared. As he and Karen unloaded crate after crate of foodstuffs and other camping supplies, I couldn't help but marvel. They must have been just as much in a panic as I was (perhaps more so, given they wouldn't have started until after the bombs dropped), yet had clearly thought this through in much more depth. How had they accumulated so much while pandemonium rained around them? It was a thought that fed my suspicion.

It wasn't just the food and what seemed like several gallons of water. They had cutlery, utensils, proper tools, a small electric stove and several lamps. But they still had a lot to learn about the essentials. A generator and fuel to run it were a heavy luxury that took up a lot of space on their trailer. I said nothing though. The harsh realities of island life would soon become obvious.

As I carried some of the last items down the

dock, the children who up until then had been helping where they could, were flagging.

'Mummy, I'm tired' Aileen, the little girl said.

'I know sweetie, we'll rest soon I promise. Just a few more things.'

'Why don't you and the others head up with the kids? Your Husband and I can manage the rest' I said.

'Thank you' she said, trying her best at a small smile. She went to leave and then turned back. 'And thanks again. You know… for this.'

It was my turn to try and force a smile.

She gathered the kids and a few last items and set off up the slope. I stood watching them go. They didn't look dangerous and I felt silly for being so paranoid. But as Steve passed them on his way back from the house, they stopped. I could see them talking in hushed tones and glancing in my direction. I pretended not to notice, busying myself rearranging the rifle strap around my chest. At length, they broke up. It looked like they had reached agreement on something, although on what, I had no idea. I could feel a chill on the back of my neck. It could be innocent, or it could all be a ruse. They outnumbered me seven to one (well, five adults to one) and could just be waiting for the right moment. I resolved again to remain cautious.

Jake came over the side of the boat loaded with two crates one atop the other. I trudged back up the dock to get them.

'Just the barrels and the generator left' he said.

I nodded.

'How robust are the barrels?' I asked. 'Could they be rolled?'

'Yeah, for sure. Although, we'd want to be careful on this old wood.' He stamped his foot. 'It doesn't inspire confidence'

This made me smile in spite of myself. He was absolutely right, it didn't.

Steve arrived at the shore and slowed his pace as he reached us, making sure not to breach the six-feet rule.

'So, I was thinking: You guys unload the barrels and I'll roll them one by one down the dock. Once they're all there we'll push them up them up as far as the first house. We can store them under the eave at the back for the time being. Then we'll come back for the generator and the last two crates'

Jake hesitated before responding.

'Well, we'll probably want at least a couple of them up by the generator.'

It occurred to me that if we left them at the first house, I would be between them and their fuel and their boat. It wasn't my motivation, I was just dog tired from shifting all the gear. But I could see where he was coming from.

'Yes, that makes sense. Hey we can roll them all up there if you want. I just thought you might be as tired as I am?'

'I guess we can always bring them the rest of the way up tomorrow?' he looked at Steve, a silent conversation passing between them.

'Yeah, suits me.' Steve looked more tired than I was and I think he was relieved that Jake gave in.

We set to it. The barrels were beastly and heavier than I'd imagined. It took several minutes for the guys to offload the first one and several more for me to get it onto its side and roll it down the dock to the shore. The old wood underfoot creaked in agony as I went, sounding as if it was putting in almost as much effort as I was. By the time we'd done the first two, we had all dispensed with our outer wear and were sweating through our t-shirts.

The idea of having an electricity source was enticing, but I wasn't exactly sure it would be useful. Powering lamps in the evening might be something, but I wasn't sure it was worth all the effort.

The last barrel came over and the guys set about untying the generator. I shoved it towards the beach, rolling it along the dock. Suddenly, the rhythmic creaking of wood became an angry crack and the barrel and I broke clear through the dock and plunged into the water below.

In shock at the cold, my breath shot from my lungs. I flung my arms in a wide arc to get to the surface, but something was holding me back. I glanced downwards in panic, the salt stinging my eyes. My foot was wedged under the barrel. My head was just half a metre from the surface, but I couldn't reach it.

I bent down and heaved at it, but with the additional weight of several gallons of sea-water now on top of it, it wouldn't shift. Adrenaline and fear shot through my veins. I pulled viciously at my leg, desperate for freedom. My lungs were bursting and my chest spasmed for air.

A shadow appeared above me and was followed by a parting of the water as Jake appeared next to me. He saw my foot and pointed at the barrel.

Together we managed to move it just enough to free my foot. I lunged for the surface, coughing and spluttering as my head broke clear. A firm pair of arms grabbed me under the shoulders and heaved me upwards.

It was Steve. He managed to get my chest clear of the water and pulled me back on top of him. We both lay there on the dock panting, as Jake hauled himself out of the water. Next to us was a large hole where a part of the old wooden dock used to be.

My head cleared in an instant and I reached back for the gun. It was gone. I rolled over and pushed myself up, staggering backwards from them.

Steve was surprised by my sudden motion and nearly fell over the side himself. As he steadied I looked from him to Jake. They were both still sitting on the dock and breathing heavily.

Jake was looking down at his lap. And in hands was the rifle.

4

Back at the big house, Maisie helped her sister Karen put the two children to bed. In a small room at the top of the stairs they laid out two camp beds and spread sleeping bags out on top of them.

'What happens now mum?' asked Tom, the older of the two children.

'We're going to be fine love,' she said, although she didn't sound as convincing as she would have liked.

The kids lay down without protest, exhausted from their long journey.

'Mummy, who's that man?' asked Aileen. Karen hesitated. Maisie replied for her.

'He lives here. He's been very kind to let us stay here with him.'

'Get some rest now you two. Aunty Maisie and I will be just downstairs.'

They pulled the door to the jam, leaving a

small space just the way the kids liked it, and headed down into the front room. Steve's wife Susan was there, staring out the window. They collapsed into the old armchairs next to her, clouds of dust from the old cushions circling them.

'So what do you think?' asked Karen.

'About Carl?' Maisie replied. 'I'm not sure yet. He looks pretty wild with that scruffy beard and unkempt hair, but he's been here alone and I think we just startled him. I don't think he means any harm.'

'I'm not so sure,' Susan interjected. 'I mean, he seemed pretty keen *not* to have any company.'

'I honestly didn't think we'd find anyone up in these remote parts. I wonder how long he's been here?'

Maisie's question hung in the air between them, unanswered.

They sat like that for a few minutes, listening to the strange quiet of the island. Now that the frenzied activity of unloading the boat was complete and the kids were sleeping, the shock of their arrival had begun to set it.

Finally, Karen spoke:

'So this is it then. Our new home. A rock in the ocean with an armed man as host.'

'I guess so,' said Maisie. 'Anywhere but back where we came from, I suppose.'

Karen nodded slowly.

'I honestly didn't think we'd get here. Especially without...' she stopped, a tear forming in her eye.

'The important thing is that we're safe now. Well, at least we should be safe. As long as Carl isn't a nut-job…' said Maisie

They laughed in unison. But it was a grim laugh, laced with uncertainty.

'Are either of you hungry, thirsty?' asked Karen

'I'm not sure what I am,' said Susan. Maisie nodded.

'Yeah… I know what you mean. I wonder what's taking the boys so long?'

Just at that moment they heard footsteps approaching. They rose to their feet and went out to the hall, just as Steve, was coming through the front door. Susan went to him and hugged him.

As Jake followed him in behind, they were startled by Karen's raised voice from behind them.

'How did you get that?!'

They all looked at Jake. He looked down at the rifle he was carrying.

'What happened to Carl?' asked Maisie.

5

I stood staring at Jake holding my rifle, waiting for his next move. But Jake just sat there, staring at the gun. Steve's eyes were focused on Jake too.

I wondered if I could make it to their boat in time. It was behind me though and I didn't want to risk taking my eyes off Jake to assess the distance.

My mind moved to the hunting knife stashed with the fishing equipment, just inside the door of my little house. Between that weapon and me was a long run and two men I didn't know. And one of them had the most dangerous weapon on the island.

None of us spoke. I don't think any of us had expected this confrontation. At least, not at this time and in this way.

I considered making a lunge for the gun. I didn't think Steve would be quick enough to stop me, but if he got in the way even slightly, it would give Jake enough time to lift the gun. I couldn't risk it.

Jake continued to sit there. He looked up at

Steve and then back down again to the rifle. It looked to me like he wasn't sure what to do next. That may have been a good thing, but I needed an idea quickly, in case he was deciding whether to shoot me or not. My mind raced.

I looked out the corner of my eye to the rocky outcrop that the dock was attached to on the shore line. *A loose rock*, I thought. *Something to throw at him and give me the brief second I need.* And in the same moment, *He just saved your life, why would he shoot you?*

Steve noticed me glancing towards the rocks.

'Jake…' he said.

Jake looked up at him again and then towards me.

'Mister,' he said. 'Carl, I mean. We meant it when we said we meant you no harm.'

I was almost relieved at this, but I could feel a 'but' coming. A pit opened up in my stomach.

'My family,' he continued. 'The kids. It's nothing personal. We don't know you and I think we'd all feel safer if I kept hold of the gun.'

Ok, I thought. *He just wants to keep hold of the gun. He doesn't know about the knife. I can use it to get the rifle back later.*

I cleared my throat. It's easy to be brave when you've got the guns. Much harder without. It was time for another leap of faith.

'I understand. And thank you. For saving me.' I pointed at the water. He nodded.

'We really are good people.' He seemed almost

remorseful about keeping the gun.

'Perhaps you should go and rest with your family. I could do with a break too.' I said. All I could think about was getting back to my house and reassessing the situation. With my knife in hand.

'Yeah. I think we've all had enough excitement for one morning. Why don't you head up later this afternoon? We have… a lot to discuss.'

'Ok,' I agreed.

Jake lifted himself up, leaning on the gun for support. Steve joined him. They left slowly, backing away at first before turning and heading up to the shore.

I stood there a moment longer, considering my options.

With them gone I could grab a few things from home and steal away in their boat. Or I could wait it out and see what happened. Potentially I could take them by surprise at some point and get my gun back.

I was angry with myself for letting this happen. I'd come so far, been so careful, but still I'd lost the upper hand.

If I were to sail off in their boat, where would I go? It was certainly a sturdier vessel then my own, but I didn't have any map or idea where any other islands might be. Judging by their determination to stay, going back to the mainland was not an option.

If I left it would mean losing everything I had accomplished here. The relative comfort I had found for myself. I would be leaving behind immediate survival for immediate uncertainty. And there was something else too.

These people seemed like good enough folk. I'd spent many hours fearing the arrival of other people. But now they were here, I realised how lonely I'd been. Living here alone was one thing, but there was additional safety and comfort to be had in living here with others. Especially if they turned out to be allies.

No, I would stay. If the opportunity came to reacquire the gun then I would. But for now, I would watch and wait. And carry the knife with me. Just in case.

6

Back at home I sat at the table, hungry but unable to eat. I turned the morning's events over in my head.

In all my plans for the future I hadn't pictured living with others on this island. And yet, here they were. It was all quiet, except for the sound of the waves hitting the shore. I could almost imagine I was still alone. But they were up there, setting up home in the big house.

I wondered what they were doing right now and what they were thinking. I wondered what they thought of me. I got up and looked at my reflection in the window. It was a shock.

The face I remembered, the one I'd stared into every morning since I started shaving, was unrecognisable. I hadn't shaved since I'd arrived on the island and a full beard covered the lower-half of my face. My hair was scruffy and unkempt. I just hadn't felt the need to comb it. There were bags under my eyes to go with some new wrinkles.

But most surprising of all, was the coldness in my eyes. I looked hardened, angry even. The younger, less troubled version of me was gone, replaced by an older more severe version. A version who had learned some painful truths about survival. Was it any wonder that the newcomers felt fear at the sight of this man, let alone the gun he carried? Did this still give me some advantage? If so, it wouldn't last much longer. Plus, it could lead to them deciding to get rid of me.

Jake had saved my life. But he had also kept the gun. What did that mean? Was he genuinely concerned for the safety of his group, or was he just trying to build up the nerve to use it on me? There were so many questions. They bounced around my head until I choked in exasperation.

There were things that needed doing around the island. I needed to go on another water run. But I felt trapped inside my little house. It was all so strange. What would I say if I bumped into them? Would they suspect me of something nefarious?

I decided I would accept Jake's invitation to join them at the big house for a conversation. I would let them rest a while longer and then take up some tinned fruit or something. But first I needed to clean myself up.

For the first time in a very long while, I was conscious of my appearance. Not that there's was immaculate. But I had made the decision to allow these people to stay. I had done so because they seemed genuine and because in truth, I had felt the loneliness and isolation of the island creeping up on me. Now I realised, I wanted them to like me. Or at the very least, be comfortable with me. And the first step to that was being a bit more presentable.

I washed, put on a clean set of clothes and brushed my hair to the best of my ability. It was too long and still looked a bit wild, but it would have to do.

With a bit of time still to kill I switched on the radio and turned the dial back and forth, scanning for a station. There was nothing as usual, just the endless hiss of white noise. My best source of any news for now would be the new arrivals.

When I couldn't wait any longer, I tucked the knife into the waistband of my trousers and headed out the door.

7

As I walked up through the village towards the big house, I kept my eyes peeled for any activity. There was none that I could make out.

I thought of my own reckless arrival. I was so tired and distraught I'd fallen asleep on the shore. They were probably just as exhausted from their own flight. I stopped a few metres short of the front door and listened for any signs of life. Nothing.

As I stood there, the door opened and Jake appeared.

'Everything ok Carl?' he said. He must have seen me from the window.

'Yes, fine,' I said, startled. 'I didn't want to disturb you if you were resting'.

'The others are sleeping. I tried but couldn't. Why don't you come in?' he stood aside and beckoned me in. He wasn't carrying the gun.

I nodded and went inside, following him to the front room. We sat in a pair of the old armchairs facing each other. I scanned the room. They'd put some crates in the corner but there was no gun. *He's hidden it somewhere,* I thought.

I looked at him, this tall greying man in his late-forties. Who was he, I wondered. He no doubt wondered the same about me.

'Is it your boat?' I asked. It was the first thing that came to mind.

'No, I wish. It's Steve's. Was that yours up on the beach?'

'Yes,' I said.

'You came all the way here in that?' he was surprised.

'It was all I could get a hold of at short notice.'

Jake nodded and seemed to understand. There were two big questions I wanted answered: how did they know about the island and did anyone know they had come here? I approached them cautiously, so as not to sound too aggressive.

Jake stared at the ground for a moment before answering. When he did, it came out in a stream of consciousness and in a taut and pained voice.

'Karen's brother Duncan knew about the place. When it all… kicked off, he called us in the middle of the night and begged us to convince Steve to bring us all here in his boat.

We were all in shock, but he was raving like a madman. We told him to calm down and come over, which he did. He told us all about the island, how he'd seen it in some nature documentary and looked it up on a map.

At the time nobody knew how bad it was going to be. We were more worried about the fallout from the bombs than anything else. Duncan kept talking about all the post-apocalyptic shows he was into. Man turning against man sort of stuff. But we just didn't think it would come to that, not really. Whenever tragedy had struck in the past, it tended to bring people together didn't it?'

I nodded. I had been running both from nuclear fallout myself and the fall of society it would bring with it.

Jake continued:

'Anyway, at first it wasn't too bad. It was tense and frightening but people carried on. The north of Scotland has always felt very far from everywhere else. But then more bombs fell. It was full-scale nuclear war. There were pictures on the news of devastation from all over the world. Survivors from down south fled in their droves to Scotland. The police and army were on the streets but everyday there seemed to be less and less of them. The supermarkets ran dry and that's when the trouble really started.

Even then we didn't realise how bad it was going to get. Duncan kept pleading with us to run. We agreed to stockpile our supplies just in case and Steve made sure that the boat was fueled up and ready to go.

The TV stations were showing less and less frequent programming. Eventually the news was the only show broadcast, and only for an hour each night. And then that went too.

There was a breakout at the local prison and that was the turning point for us. Hardened criminals were roaming the streets with no one to stop them. The looting and mugging that had occurred already, quickly escalated to home break-ins and robbery. We lived in a small village and up to that point hadn't experienced some of the worst atrocities.'

Jake had to stop to clear a lump in his throat. Maisie appeared at the door, probably woken by our voices. She was surprised to see me sitting there but covered it well.

'Hi Carl,' she said. 'Are you ok Jake? Can I get you a glass of water?'

'Thank you yes. I'm just telling Carl about what happened' he replied.

'Carl?' she offered.

'Yes please, that would be great'

She went off to the kitchen and I urged Jake to carry on.

'There was a guy being held in the prison. Tim, he was called. He'd grown up in the same village as us and everybody knew him. He was an ex-copper who had been put inside for corruption and extortion of victims. He was a real nasty piece of work. Once he got out he went about putting a gang of thugs together. They would ride around in this old pickup truck with a Jolly Roger hanging from a pole at the back and demand "taxes" from people. Called themselves the Pirates. They took whatever they wanted. If anyone stood up to them they were either severely beaten or killed.

There were other competing gangs, but they were by far the worst and eventually they began to dominate. By this point Karen, Maisie, the kids and I had moved into Duncan's farmhouse out in the sticks. It was remote enough that we hoped we'd avoid the gangs. My sister Susan and her husband Steve moved in shortly after.

We finally agreed to Duncan's plan and had scrabbled together enough supplies. We planned to head to the port in the dead of night, to reduce the risk of being caught enroute. It was late on in the evening of the day we were due to go, when the gang found us. We heard them coming before we saw them.'

Maisie returned, handing a drink to Jake and one to me. I thanked her and she smiled briefly, before taking the seat next to Jake.

'Don't let me interrupt' she said.

'So, before we could react, Duncan grabbed his keys and raced for the door. He told us he would distract them while we got away and meet us at the port later. We tried to stop him but he wouldn't hear it. He made us promise that if he wasn't at the port by midnight we would go without him. He said he'd find another way to get to the island.

He jumped into his car and sped off towards the truck. We watched between gaps in the curtains as he hurtled towards them. They were taken by surprise and pulled out of his way just in time. He continued off down the road and they turned and gave chase.

After we were sure they weren't coming back, we loaded up the supplies and drove to the dock. We waited there until about 1am but there was no sign of him.'

Maisie was struggling to hold back tears. Jake put a hand on her shoulder.

'You don't have to go on if you don't want to, I think I get the picture,' I said.

'It's ok. You have a right to know,' he said. He took a deep slug of water before going on.

'It was becoming obvious that Duncan wasn't going to make it. We didn't know what had happened to him, but most likely they caught up with him.

None of us wanted to leave without him but the waiting felt increasingly futile. But Karen refused to let us go. Her and Duncan have always been very close and she couldn't stand the thought of leaving him there. It had been his idea after all.

Then not long after, we saw a pair of headlights crest a rise in the hills above the port. In the moonlight we could see a flag hanging from the back and we knew who it was. It stopped for a moment, just long enough to make us out by the lights on the boat I imagine. Then they came hurtling down towards us.

I forced Karen onto the boat. It was awful. She was screaming and the kids were crying. Steve fired up the boat and gunned it out to sea. The gang let off a couple of shots but by the time they got down the shore we were long gone. I don't know if they managed to steal a boat or give chase, but we didn't see another soul until we arrived here.'

He finished the water and slumped back into

the chair. He looked exhausted.

I was horrified at the tale but glad that nobody had followed them or knew where they had gone. If we were to survive this, our island would need to remain a secret, especially from guys like Tim and his gang.

'I'm sorry' I said. It didn't seem enough.

We sat in silence for a moment, Jake and I staring at the floor and Maisie carefully appraising me from the corner of her eye.

'What about you Carl?' said Maisie, breaking the quiet. 'How long have you been here?'

It was a question I'd expected and prepared for.

'I left two days after the first missile hit,' I lied. 'I got lost and nearly drowned on the way. I couldn't believe it when I got here. I had to keep busy to avoid going into shock.'

'Two days?' she asked, surprised.

'Yes. I guess you could say I had the same fears as Duncan.'

Maisie nodded, but I couldn't be sure she believed me. Her gaze was unsettling. It felt like natural curiosity mixed with a well hidden suspicion. Her blue eyes were beautiful but piercing. I continued quickly, to deflect any further questions.

'I listened to the radio each night until the broadcasts stopped. It was terrifying. Worse even, than I thought it would be.'

'It was,' said Jake. 'Worse than any of us could

have imagined.'

'God knows how the governments survived long enough to keep bombing each other. The whole world was on fire, but they just kept on going. There can't be many cities left standing' said Maisie.

We heard noises from upstairs. The rest of the family were rousing from their makeshift beds.

'I should go,' I said, rising. 'You should try and get some rest Jake. You've had a long journey. There'll be plenty of time to discuss the island and… everything else, tomorrow'

He nodded.

'Come back for dinner later?' Maisie offered.

'I don't think so.' I said. 'You guys have had a terrible ordeal and you need to be together and recover.'

'I promised her I'd go back and look for him' said Jake, not looking up from his seat. 'It was the only way I could get Karen to stay on the boat.'

'I understand Jake. But it would be suicide.' I said.

'I know he said. I know.'

8

I left the big house with my head spinning. The accounts I'd heard of riots and roaming gangs were bad enough on the radio, but hearing about it first-hand brought it closer to home. I felt lucky to have left when I did, despite the hardships I had endured on the island.

I returned home to pick up the cool-box and then walked up the hill to the reservoir. I sat for a while on the edge, looking out over the island and into the sea beyond. It was a rare sunny summer day and the sea was calm.

Stuck way out here in isolation, it was difficult to picture the chaos on the mainland. I had left the moment the first bomb struck and managed to avoid the fallout – in both senses of the word. I felt pensive and melancholy, filled with anger, disbelief and confusion over what happened. Until I'd heard Jake's story, I'd held onto the hope that living here was a temporary solution. I would wait it out until things calmed down and the governments of the world saw sense and regained control. But it was evident now that that was never going to happen. There were no more governments, no more law and order. There would be no returning to my previous life, no more going into my office or Sunday runs in the park. That way of life was over.

It was a painful realisation of a truth I already knew in my subconscious. It brought forward all the struggles I faced trying to survive alone on a small island in the North Atlantic. It was a more frightening prospect than ever before. All of a sudden, I was glad to have company.

I looked down towards the big house. Some fear and unease still remained towards these new arrivals. They still had my gun and outnumbered me. They could still decide they would like the island to themselves. But seeing their troubled faces and hearing their story had ignited a hope inside me that they really would become allies. More than that even, I hoped they would become friends. The first real friends I'd had in a very long time.

I had planted enough food to support us all, but it would be a while until it was ready. They certainly seemed to have enough supplies to last them until the crops came good. But we would need to plan carefully for the longer term. We couldn't be in a situation where one failed crop cycle left us starving.

With my thoughts now turning to food, I decided to do some early evening fishing. If I caught enough, I could offer them some as a welcome gift. A gesture of goodwill.

I took the long tramp home, carrying my water

with me. I had a long, cool drink and then collected my fishing gear and headed out to my boat. The barrels were still sat at the end of the dock where we'd left them and Steve's boat bobbed up and down by the dock.

It really was a perfect day to be out on the ocean. The sun still shone brightly, the breeze was gentle and the sea was calm. It was a little moment of paradise, despite the situation.

It took some time to catch the first fish, but once that came in I was inundated. It was by far my most successful catch since I first went out. I caught nine sea trout and another smaller fish that I didn't recognise.

Returning to shore I caught Maisie watching me from the dock. She wasn't alone, Jake and Steve were busy unloading the generator. The barrels were gone. Once I noticed her watching, she glanced away. But there was something in that look that I couldn't place.

I rowed in just as they got the generator to the end of the dock.

'Ahoy!' said Maisie. It was a friendly greeting and felt genuine.

I waved back and smiled. I jumped out and dragged the boat up the beach to its usual resting place.

'I've caught some fish. There's enough for all of us,' I said and held up my catch with a ridiculous pride.

'Wow, that's quite the haul' said Steve, wiping

his brow.

'Trust me, it isn't always that easy,' I said. 'Some days I'll be out there for hours and come back with nothing more than a goldfish for my troubles.'

Jake almost smiled. His face was still taught and troubled and he couldn't quite manage it.

I had tied the fish onto separate lines and handed eight of these to Maisie.

'This is very kind of you,' she said. 'Are you sure?'

'Yes, of course. One is more than enough for me. I trust you know what to do with them?'

'Oh yeah,' said Steve. 'I'm a keen fisherman myself. Hence the boat.'

'In that case there's probably a lot I can learn from you. So far I've pretty much been prepping them through trial and error.'

'Are you sure you won't join us?' Maisie offered again.

'Not tonight,' I said. 'Maybe tomorrow. It's been a long day for all of us.'

'You can say that again' said Jake. It was good natured but he still couldn't manage a smile. It felt like he carried the weight of his family's safety on his shoulders.

We said our goodbyes and made our way up the bank to our new homes. Jake and Steve carried the generator between them. I wondered if they planned on using it that evening. It would probably be easier for them to use the electric stove they'd brought then trying to light a fire.

Shutting the door behind me I had the sudden sense of being alone again. After all this time by myself I found I was almost craving the company. The feeling surprised me.

It was the right thing to do though. They would need time to come to terms with their situation, just as I would. I felt that sharing the fish with them had been a step in the right direction. Things would be awkward for a while, but I felt there was the definite potential of developing a rapport with them. That would have to do for now.

As the fish was cooking on the camping stove, I again checked through the radio dial. Still nothing. Would there ever be again? I doubted it, especially after hearing Jake's story.

But what of my story? I couldn't tell them the truth. They would never understand. And how could they trust me if they found out I knew it was going to happen before it did? I doubted Maisie would let me get away with the short version I had shared earlier though. She had a curious mind that one.

I made short work of my meal and sat at the window looking up into the village as the sun set. I couldn't see the big house from where I was but I could imagine them up there, cooking, contemplating and trying to come to terms with their arrival. It was a difficult thing to do, as I knew very well. But I would help them, if I could.

That night I woke several times. At night, our smallest fears can become overwhelming nightmares.

Despite everything so far pointing to my new arrivals being good people, I imagined every sound to be them breaking in to catch me off guard.

I slept with the knife under my sleeping bag and a chair lodged against the front door. Even so I spent much of the night staring at the ceiling, ready to jump up and defend myself.

9

Having spent most of the night awake, I had finally fallen into a deep slumber around dawn. I awoke much later to a sharp knock on the door. I roused myself as best I could, my head stinging. I dressed quickly and tucked the knife into my waistband before answering.

Maisie stood there, looking uncertain but with a bright smile. It was a blustery morning and her shoulder length brown hair flew freely around her face.

'Good morning,' she said. 'Sorry if I disturbed you. We've got the generator running and are frying up some of that fish with powdered eggs for breakfast. Susan does amazing things with powdered eggs. If you fancy it?'

Eggs, I thought. *It has been a while.* Even though only powdered, my mouth watered at the very mention of them.

'That would be… amazing,' I stumbled.

'Great, come up and join us when you're ready' she said, before smiling again and shooting back off up the hill.

I watched her go for a moment, still in a haze. *Is this a gesture or a trap?* I wondered. Not necessarily a trap to cause me harm, but to question me further.

As if sensing this thought she turned and caught me gazing at her. I ducked back inside humiliated. *She sees all that woman,* my mind warned me.

The thought of scrambled eggs overrode my embarrassment and it wasn't long before I was back at the big house. It would be fair to say I had arrived there almost at a run. The door was open and I poked my head around and into an intoxicating aroma of fried fish and eggs.

In the kitchen at the end of the hall, Susan was standing at the electric cooker with a frying pan. She saw me and waved me in.

'The others are in the living room, make yourself at home and I'll bring you in some breakfast' she called.

I thanked her and went into the front room. The family was all there, seated either in the discarded armchairs or on the floor. The kids were still munching their way through the food but it looked as though the adults were just finishing up. Steve was still chewing, but he was the first to spot me and motioned for me to come and sit down.

I took a space on the floor between the chair Steve was sitting on and Jake, who was sitting on the floor. Jake nodded as he put his plate down in front of him.

'There's not a lot that scrambled eggs can't fix' Karen said. I smiled in return.

Susan came in carrying two plates, one which she handed to me. I was overwhelmed with the delicious smell and barely took a moment to thank her before tucking in.

'We don't have much powdered egg left, but I thought we might need a treat this morning. So there you go,' she said. I nodded and munched, feeling very grateful.

A quiet settled over the room. I could tell that my presence hung heavy on them, along with their new situation.

It was Tom who broke the ice.

'What's next mum?' he said.

'Are you still hungry?' asked Karen in response.

'No, I mean… what's next?'

It was a good question, which none of us had the answer for.

'Well,' I said, seizing the opportunity to make a good impression. 'There's still a lot of the island for you to see. I still need to take you up the mountain and show you the birds.'

'The birds?' he said, with a childlike curiosity. He wasn't the only one. I could see raised eyebrows from others around the room.

'Yes. There are hundreds of them, all living together at the back of the island.'

‘Are they big?’ he said

‘Well, not bigger than normal. But there are puffins up there.’

‘I’ve never seen a puffin’ said Aileen.

I didn’t have much experience with kids. I didn’t know how to relate to them at all. So I just went with the default bright and smiley voice I’d seen people using on TV and in movies. It seemed to work.

‘Well, maybe you will today,’ said Susan. She smiled at me and at the very least, I think she appreciated my effort.

We finished up breakfast and made small talk about the weather. It wasn’t a perfect day to march up the back of the island, but I remembered how important distracting myself from the reality of my arrival on the island had been. I thought it best if I could do the same for them.

I showed them the reservoir first and although I’d told them about it the day before, they were still as shocked as I first was when they saw it.

‘Can we swim in it?’ asked Tom.

I was stunned at how well the kids were taking it. But then I supposed that that was the innocence of youth. As long as their parents were nearby, they felt safe, no matter where they were. This was just another adventure. The adults were a different story. They concealed their anxiety well, but it was there behind every tight smile.

Maisie was one who seemed to be coping best in the face of it all. She must have felt as anxious as the rest of them, yet on the surface at least, it didn’t seem to phase her.

'No silly,' she said. 'That's our drinking water. But if you like, I'm sure we can take a swim in the sea some time.'

She was a marvel.

We pressed on to the top of the hill, stopping to admire the view of the village and the shore, before heading across the back of the island. I showed them the cliff where I'd inadvertently discovered the bird shit. I told them the story and it lightened the mood of everyone except Jake.

I could tell he was distracted. It felt more than just carrying the gravity of the situation with him. But it wasn't the time to ask him about it.

Finally, we skirted back up the cliffs so I could show them the birds. We lay at the top, peering over the edge.

'I've been thinking of this place as "Bird Lookout". But I suppose "The Birds Nest" would be more appropriate,' I said.

'Bird... Lookout,' Jake repeated, trailing off.

'How about "Puffin's Paradise"?' Aileen offered.

'Which ones are the Puffins?' asked Tom.

I pointed them out to him and his face shone with wonder. Maisie sat up and looked back down the island.

'This is some place to be stranded,' she said. 'We could do much worse.'

I nodded. I'd admired the beauty of the place

several times. There were much worse places to wash up.

We rested a while at the top, the kids momentarily distracted by their feathered friends. Sitting in silence we stared down towards the sea. The wind was much worse up here but if the others noticed, it didn't seem to bother them at that moment.

After a while, Karen grew tired of Tom's incessant calls to the puffins (*here puffy, puffy. Come here Mr puffy)* and declared that it was time to head back.

Steve took a light tumble on our way back, when his foot caught on a rock. It was a reminder to all of us to stay alert and not get too comfortable. We were a long way from medical attention. If such a thing even existed anymore.

Once we got back to the path, Tom sprinted ahead with Aileen trailing in his wake. Karen called out to them to slow down, but to no avail. When we arrived at the barn, I realised why he'd been so keen to run ahead. The door to the annex was open.

Oh no.

Hearing us coming, Tom appeared at the doorway.

'Hey mum,' he called. 'There's a radio in here!'

My heart caught in my throat. It was too early. Way too early.

I'd planned to move the radio down to my house before they'd had a chance to see it. I was beginning to feel that these new arrivals were trustworthy, but I still didn't want to chance them using it to broadcast our location. Jake still had my gun too and I had no way of knowing if I was being lulled into a fall sense of security. What would they think when they realised I'd lied?

But it was too late now. Karen was making a beeline for the annex, followed by the rest of them. Only Maisie stayed behind. She stood looking at me with a blank expression, as I stared after them.

10

Karen reached the doorway first and peered inside. Jake and Steve stood just behind her while Susan scolded Tom for running off.

'It is a radio!' Karen exclaimed. She sounded hopeful. And that was a bad sign.

'See for yourself,' she stood aside for the others.

Jake and Steve ventured into the small room. Maisie began making her way down towards them and I followed. We joined the small gathering as they came back out.

'It looks ancient,' said Steve. 'Probably hasn't been used in years'.

'It might work,' said Karen.

Work for what?

Jake shook his head. 'The battery is covered in grime and looks decrepit. There's no way it still works.'

'That's what I thought,' I said. They all looked at me and I flushed.

'Have you tried it?' asked Karen. She still sounded unnervingly optimistic.

'No,' I said. 'I didn't want to risk it.'

'What do you mean?' she replied.

'If by some miracle that old thing fired up, I didn't want to inadvertently send out a signal to anyone who might be listening.'

'Why did you tell us the room was empty Carl?' Maisie asked. She didn't sound angry. But the question demanded an answer and she watched me intently.

'I didn't... *I don't* know you,' I said. I had my reasons, but I still felt ashamed. 'For all I know, you could be part of a much larger group. You could be waiting for the right time to force me off the island. Or worse.'

They were all staring at me with genuine shock on their faces. All except Jake, who stared at the ground, the same grim expression on his face.

'The radio... It was too early. If you managed to use it somehow...' I shrugged.

'We might alert others to our presence,' Jake finished the thought.

'That's right,' I said. 'We're safe here. But the more people that know about the island, the less safe we are.'

'We have to at least try it,' said Karen 'If we could get in contact with the mainland, we might be able to reach Duncan.'

Jake shook his head. He looked miserable.

'No. Carl is right, it's too risky.'

I exhaled in relief. I felt like I'd been holding my breath for several minutes.

'Jake!' Karen stared at him with fury in her eyes. He shook his head again.

'I'm sorry Karen,' He turned and headed back down towards the house. Karen stormed after him. I was relieved he understood. But there would be a cost. Karen was desperate to rescue her brother but Jake knew it was futile and risky. He had to stand in the way.

There was an awkward silence as we stood in our broken circle. Even the kids were keeping quiet. They probably felt responsible for causing a rift among the adults.

'I'm sorry,' I said. 'I should have just been straight with you.'

'It's alright Carl,' Steve said. 'We understand. I think.'

I nodded my thanks.

Susan gathered herded the kids back towards the house. I hoped she had the smarts to take them to the garden or something and leave Jake and Karen well alone for a while.

'Is there anything else you… want to tell us?' asked Maisie. She picked her words carefully and it was an open question, with no hint of malice. But I felt like she didn't just mean about the island.

'No,' I said. 'There's nothing else. I would have told you about the radio eventually. I hope you believe that.'

'I do,' she said. Steve nodded too.

'I'm going to...' I couldn't think of anything so I just indicated down the slope and left. I could feel their eyes on my back as I hurried off. I kept going until I was back inside the sanctuary of my little house.

Once inside I stood staring at the ceiling. None of this was going according to plan.

It all felt so chaotic since these new people had arrived. Before they'd come I had managed to bring a semblance of order to my new life. I busied myself with chores around the island and survival in general. I was on the edge, but I felt in control. Now though, nothing felt that way.

I had let them stay because I thought I could control the situation. Take things at my own pace. But almost from the outset, when I plunged into the water and had to be rescued by Jake, it had been one misstep after another. I couldn't control this, I couldn't control them and I couldn't control how our relationship developed. And that scared me.

I closed my eyes and tried to focus on my breathing. The important thing was that they posed no threat to me. Of that I was fairly certain. They were just honest and genuine people who were on the run from a world on fire.

We could make this work together. But for them to trust me I would have to throw caution to the wind. I would have to be open and frank with them and stop trying to lead them in one direction or another. I didn't know if I could do that. But I had to try. There was no going back now.

Just then I heard the sound of heavy footsteps and there was a knock on my door. I knew it was Jake before I opened it.

He looked wretched, his face flushed red and his thin grey hair wild. In his hands, wrapped tightly with a firm grip, was my gun.

11

We are not born to mistrust. As children, we trust everyone implicitly. And why would we not? Our parents are kind to us, why would others not be?

Like reading and writing, mistrust is something that has to be learned. One of the first lessons our parents teach us is not to talk to strangers. There is danger in the unknown and we must learn this for our own safety. But the real lessons about trust are learned later in life.

We have all of us been betrayed at one time or another. We have all been let down. And with each act of disloyalty, our ability to trust is weakened. The deeper the betrayal, the harder the effect.

The older we get, the more distrustful we are likely to become. It is a simple (though sad) fact of life. Trust is difficult. But thankfully, we still want to do it.

At the heart of all of us we know that trust can lead to the greatest experiences of our lives. Love, the most enjoyable and wild of emotions, is built on trust.

It is something we aspire to.

The great Chinese philosopher Confucius said "Rulers need three resources: weapons, food and trust. The ruler who cannot have all three should give up weapons first, then food, but should hold on to trust at all costs: without trust we cannot stand." He died in 479 BC.

History is littered with great acts of Trust. But we are not as interested in them as we are in the *breakdown* of relationships. Many more books have been written about the outbreak of wars for instance, than have been about the acts that avoided them.

Nuclear destruction had been forestalled once before because of Trust. President John F. Kennedy had received two conflicting messages from Premier Nikita Khrushchev; one rolling back to avoid conflict and another threatening it. JFK had to trust that Khrushchev wanted to avoid war as much as he did, but was under pressure from the hawks in his government to fire the first shot. That single act of trust saved the world. For a little while anyway.

I cannot tell you what was in Jake's mind as he marched down to my door, rifle in hand. It may be that he knew exactly what he was going to do, or it may be that he was conflicted. Trust on the one hand, safety on the other.

My isolation and constant fear from the last few months had left me paranoid. Under any normal circumstances I would never have suspected Jake or any of the others of malice. But these were not normal times.

'I'm sorry Carl,' was all he said before lifting the gun towards me.

My body braced for the shot.

It didn't come.

My eyes were open, but after a beat I realised I wasn't actually seeing. Jake was staring at me, a confused look on his face.

'I should never have taken this. It belongs to you.'

He was trying to hand the gun back to me. I raised a hand and took it from him, lowering it to my side.

It was his turn to look nervous.

'Thank you, Jake,' I said

He nodded.

In that awkward moment of silence before he raised a hand slightly in a weak wave and left, something passed between us. An understanding. An acknowledgement of the big steps we had made toward each other. For my part, letting them stay. For his, passing over the only gun on the island to the person he knew the least.

It was trust. Unspoken and undefined, but pure and frightening and true.

It was the beginning of everything. I never feared them again.

12

Things were easier after that. It was like a great cloud of lead had been lifted from us and we could all breathe again. Each of us had held a weapon and neither of us had used it against the other. We still didn't know each other very well, but we no longer feared one another.

The next morning, we had an impromptu meeting in the front room of the big house. We talked about the things we needed to do around the island to keep on living. They defaulted to me to guide them as to what needed doing, which was understandable. I'd had months to get used to my new life on the island, whereas they had only just arrived and were just as breathless and uncertain as I was in my first few days.

I talked them through my daily routines; tending to the crops, making water runs, fishing, renovations. We discussed dividing up the tasks and agreed to plant out more crops, now there were more of us to help. They agreed with me that figuring out an easier way to get water down to the village would be beneficial. They had some renovations of their own to do on the big house, which brought us around to talking about another issue – our lack of wood.

We discussed it for some time but couldn't arrive at many solutions. The best idea we could come up with was tearing down the barn and using the wood from there. Jake suggested we all give it some more thought and discuss it at a later date.

The discussion went on for several hours. Just as we were winding up and assigning tasks Karen mentioned one last thing.

'Duncan,' she said. 'What about my brother?'

Jake sighed.

'We'll go back love. Just give us a week or so to settle in and figure out a plan.'

Karen knew he was putting it off. We all did. But it had been a long morning and she let it go. I could tell from the uneasy air that often settled between her and Jake, that it was not the last time she mentioned it.

We fell into a groove. Although now headed towards the end of summer, the weather was unseasonably warm. Especially for an island in the far North Atlantic. I never spoke of it, but at the back of my mind an image of a world ablaze in nuclear fire was ever present. Was that the reason or was it just coincidence? Were we as safe from the radiation up here as I'd thought when I first made my plans? We had no way of knowing and nothing to do about it if we weren't. So, it went unspoken. The mushroom cloud in every room.

The wealth of supplies they had brought with them gave us some comfort. Although we were all conscious of our need to preserve them as best we could, until the crops bore fruit. They had brought plenty of fuel for the boat and the generator with them too. Jake and I ventured out once, taking a wide northerly arc out from the island, in search of another outcrop which might contain a tree or two. All we found however, was more ocean. We were loath to waste any more fuel on another search, but knew we would have to someday.

As time wore on the others began to adjust. They were led by Tom and Aileen, who as children, found adapting to their surroundings all the easier. One afternoon I offered to take them fishing. They jumped at the chance. Maisie offered to come with us and Karen gave the ok.

It was the calmest day yet on the island. There were no clouds in the sky and the afternoon sun shone bright and reflected off the deep blue water with a clarity that made us wince.

'I want to drive!' Tom said, as we neared my old boat.

'You can drive if you want Tom,' I replied 'But we're not using the engine. This boat will be man-powered!'

He looked confused.

'I'll show you once we get out there,' I said.

We all tugged the boat down to the water and I held it knee deep in the cool water, as they splashed about getting in.

I rowed us a short way out before saying 'Right then Tom, time to drive,' and motioning for him to swap seats with me in the middle of the boat. He had never rowed before but gave it his best shot. I can't say that we went anywhere other than around in a few circles, but we congratulated him all the same.

Maisie took over. She was even more determined than the boy and to be fair, a lot more coordinated. She pulled hard and was exhausted after a few minutes, but she'd taken us out a good distance from the island. I pulled the oars in and she collapsed at the front of the boat with a smile on her face.

I retrieved the lines and tackle from my pack and we set about trying to catch some fish. The first hour was fruitless though and the kids grew bored and hot from the sun, their enthusiasm waning. Tom leaned over the side and splashed water over Aileen, who shrieked.

'Tom!' Maisie said, stern but not unkind. 'Be nice to your sister'.

I don't know what I was thinking in the moment, but keen to entertain the kids after the disappointment of the fishing, I reached over myself and caught Maisie with a good splash of cold sea water. Maisie yelped and the kids opened up in peels of laughter.

Getting over her shock fast, Maisie set a determined look, cupped both hands over the side and launched her own assault in my direction. I attempted to shield myself from the deluge with my hands. When it hit me, I feigned agony and tipped myself over the side, plunging into the cold but refreshing water.

Looking back up at the boat I could see Maisie was a bit alarmed, but the children were besides themselves and laughing in that uncontrollable, free way that only children can. I held the boat with one arm and stretched out the other, launching a tirade of water in their direction.

The boat bobbed and swayed as they beat a hasty retreat to the other side. Maisie grabbed the bucket which was supposed to store our catch and made to dump its contents on my head. I plunged my head under just in time. When I rose to the surface again, all three of them were now in fits of laughter.

'Truce?' I called out. Maisie nodded, still smiling.

'To be honest, you're the wettest one of all of us. So, I'd say we win!'

I clambered back on board.

'Shall we head back?' I asked.

'No,' she said. 'Let's give it another half-an-hour or so. Give us a chance to dry out and see if we can't catch at least one fish to take back with us.'

The kids, spirits lifted by our water fight, were happy to stay.

We fished for another twenty minutes before Aileen finally caught a nibble. Tom helped her haul the little fish aboard and I refilled the bucket, unhooked it and released it into the fresh water.

Aileen was thrilled. She sat over the bucket watching the fish, while Tom relaunched her line, clearly deciding it was luckier than his and determined to catch one of his own.

The first fish of the day brought us a bit more luck. Tom caught two more and Maisie almost caught something very big indeed, until the line broke and it got away. Happy with our success and with the sun heading into the far western horizon, we made our way back. The current had taken us a fair distance out from the island and it was a hard slog back for me at the oars, but for the first time in a very long while, I felt content. Maisie matched my smile with her own, as the kids dosed in her lap. For a few hours at least, we were free of the intensity and pressure of our new lives. It felt like a holiday.

Back on dry land Tom and Aileen showed off their catch with immense pride. Karen, who hadn't really expected them to catch anything at all, but was grateful for the break, beamed with pleasure.

'Well that's dinner sorted,' she said. 'If only we had some chips to go with it.'

'Give it a few months and we will,' I said. Caught up in the moment, I was feeling optimistic. We would have potatoes for sure, but *frying* them would be another matter.

It was an evening to remember. The children's excitement from their first fishing trip was infectious and Susan, Jake and Karen listened with patience as they retold the story to each of them in turn, while Steve, Maisie and I prepared and cooked the fish.

We sat around the front room eating and talking. The children were exhausted and were put to bed soon after we finished. Steve slipped out the room with a grin and came back shortly after with something I hadn't seen in a very long time: Beer. Three whole bottles of Budweiser. It was a revelation.

We poured them into cups and sat contently, drinking them slowly and savouring every sip. It was the first time any of us had felt relaxed in several months. For one night at least, we felt normal again.

As the sun set and night fell upon us, I said my goodbyes and left them to it. I hadn't got more than a few feet away when I heard Maisie call out to me from the doorway.

I turned to see her coming right for me. Before I had a chance to think, she flung her arms around me. 'Thank you, Carl. For everything'. It was a brief hug and then she was gone.

I stood looking at the closed door for a moment, feeling surprised, confused and foolish all at the same time. With nothing else for it, I turned and headed back down the slope. *I didn't hug her back,* I thought. I thought the same thing over and over as I lay in my bed that night. Until it dawned on me that the most interesting thing was not that I hadn't, but that I'd wished I had.

She had no way of knowing it, but that hug was the first I'd had since I was a young child.

13

One morning, Karen rose early while the rest of us slept. She had gone to sleep with a single thought in her head which she repeated over and over again until she drifted off: *4am. I will wake up at 4am.*

There were no alarm clocks on the island and even if there had been, she wouldn't have used one. She wanted to wake up before the rest of us. And with enough time to do what she needed to do.

It was still dark outside when her eyelids fluttered open at around 3:50. She lay still on her foam camping mattress and listened. Jake snored softly beside her, but there were no other sounds save for the rhythmic crash of sea against rock.

Jake wasn't a heavy sleeper, but he wasn't a light one either. She planned to tell him that nature was calling if he woke, but wasn't sure she would still have the nerve to execute her plan if he did. She moved slowly, first sitting, then crouching and finally standing upright. Jake stirred but didn't wake. *Good,* she thought. *That's the first hurdle covered.*

Stepping lightly, she made her way out of the room, pausing to look back once more at Jake. He hadn't moved.

The stairs were tricky. They were old and creaky and right by the kids' room. If they heard anything at all they were liable to investigate or at the very least, call out for their mother.

She stood at the top, peering down at them. She'd practiced several routes down over the last few days, trying to remember the worst places. Her heart hammered in her chest and she struggled to think clearly. She tried to deepen her breathing. *It's all still explainable at this point,* she thought. *Couldn't sleep that's all. Thought I'd make a coffee. Tried not to wake you, sorry.*

She turned sideways and placed a foot on the top step, heel pressed back against the wall. The stairs mostly creaked in the middle. The edges were less well-worn and were strengthened by the joins. She placed her weight down gradually. The wood gave a soft groan, but no loud crack or creak. She exhaled. *This might be ok.*

One by one she took the steps the same way, heel pressed back and weight applied gradually. With each step she grew in confidence, but with three to go, the stair beneath her foot gave a loud creak. She paused and held her breath, listening for any sound of movement. Her heart rang in her ears so loud that she was sure the others must hear it.

After several moments of nervous agony, she was reassured that none had woken and continued.

She reached the bottom without further incident.

She made her way out through the kitchen to the back door, which she had left propped open the night before. The handle and lock mechanism were in bad need of oil and gave a horrific squeal whenever they were used. So, she'd made sure she was the last one up and left it open. She'd also left a flashlight on the windowsill.

Out in the garden she reached behind the generator and pulled out a small but heavy metal box. She'd been careful bringing it down here and even more careful cleaning it. They only used the generator sparingly for cooking and so she had hidden the box as best she could and waited for as long as she dare.

She didn't know much about electronics, but a flat battery in her car years ago and a jump start from a kind stranger, had taught her that red connected to red and black to black. It wasn't rocket science.

Karen had no way of knowing if it would work. The battery didn't look damaged, it had been protected from the elements in its little cabin after all, but it was very old. *Only one way to find out,* she told herself.

She made her way up the short slope to the barn, carrying the battery with both arms, the flashlight in her mouth. When she reached the small outhouse, she turned and looked back down behind her. No signs of movement. *Ok,* she thought. *So far, so good. Even if I get caught now, at least I'll know if it works.*

She went into the little room and closed the door behind her. Then she sat in the chair and reached under the desk, connecting the wires up carefully. *Black first, then red.*

There were no sparks, no signs of life. She didn't know if that was a bad sign or not, but thought it probably was.

She placed the headphones over her head and the microphone in front of her. Then she looked at the radio. There were two large dials on the front, but there didn't appear to be an *on* switch. *How do you turn this damn thing on?,* she thought as she felt around the back for a switch. Nothing.

Frustration began to seep in. She had taken a lot of time to plan and prepare for this moment. She was prepared for the battery to be useless, but not for the inability to switch the damn thing on and find out.

In quiet exasperation, she reached out and twisted the dials. The first one did nothing but the second produced a small clicking sound. She twisted it back and heard the click again. Was that how it worked?

There was no visible change to the radio when the click sounded. She moved the flashlight closer and inspected the dial. Around the edge was a faded thin line which grew in thickness the further round it went. A pointer on the dial indicated that the clicking sound occurred when the dial was on the far left, at the thin edge of the line. *Volume!* she thought. So that's how you turn it on.

Her triumph was short lived though. She turned the dial all the way to the right but the radio still gave no indication that it was on or working.

She grabbed the flashlight and looked down at the battery. It all seemed to be connected up right. She reached down and tugged at the live wire to be sure.

Suddenly the silence in the room was split open with a howl of white noise. She jumped up, sending the chair crashing back against the wall. The room was silent again but her ears were on fire from the shock. Adrenaline coursed through her veins, making her skin feel alive to every sensation.

She regained her composure and tried to calm down. She checked outside for signs of life. The sun hadn't risen yet, but a dim grey light perched on the horizon, signaling its imminent return. There were no signs of movement from the big house.

She returned to her place at the desk and turned the dial back to the far left, but not far enough to click the radio off. Then she tugged and twisted the wire again. The radio hissed intermittently, albeit at a much lower volume. She kept twisting the wire around in small movements until finally, the hiss became a steady stream.

With her heart pounding hard against her chest, she turned the other dial, searching for any kind of signal. The sound from the headphones ebbed, flowed and crackled, but despite several slow rotations, she found nothing. *Only one thing for it,* she thought.

She began at one end of the spectrum, pressing the button on the microphone and reciting the message she had practiced in her head and learned by heart.

"My name is Karen. I am with my family on a small island to the north of Scotland. I am trying to reach my brother Duncan, who was last seen on the mainland. If anyone can hear me, please respond."

She waited two minutes before turning the dial slightly and repeating the process. She continued trying for as long as she dared, before the sun fully came up and awoke the others from their slumber. But there was nothing.

She would try again the next morning. And the next. It would be quite some time before she finally got a response.

END OF PART TWO

PART THREE

1

Not long after our fishing trip (and shortly before Karen began her secret vigils), the weather took a turn for the worse. Thick grey clouds filled the skies and settled in like stubborn gods. There were frequent thunderstorms and it rained in hard bursts, as though the clouds themselves were angry at the earth.

The air took on a dense, hazy quality. The sun, on the rare occasion it appeared, seemed weak and emitted a dim yellow light which scarcely touched the ground. The temperature plummeted and went on slipping downwards as the days wore on.

Our honeymoon period was over and the harsh reality of life on a remote island in the North Atlantic took hold. We were wet and windswept. We had all brought warm clothes and weatherproofs to the island, but without central heating to rewarm us every night, the cold became a constant gnawing sensation that seeped into our bones.

It was as if mother nature had forgotten

autumn, with the seasons switching at once from summer to winter. Or at least, that's what we hoped. If this was autumn, we feared what winter would bring.

Our crops, which had been growing steadily before, became sluggish. They still grew and did not want for water, but without a steady stream of sunlight their development was stilted.

Fishing was much harder. The sea had turned to menacing shades of black and dark blue and the waves grew high and fierce. The birds took shelter in caves and inlets further down the cliff and were much harder to catch. We began to rely more heavily on our own supplies and with each discarded tin, were reminded that they would not last forever.

We started work on a small channel that would allow us to filter water down from the reservoir to a small catchment area we had dug across the path from the dome. Our idea was to build a miniature sluice gate, which we could open to set the water flowing down the hill and close again when the catchment was full. In principle it would work, but the only source of wood we had was from the walls of the barn and much of it was weathered and rotting.

We continued digging anyway, planning to go in search of more wood when the weather improved (If it ever did). It was grim, slow work. We had some good tools that the others had brought with them, but a shovel was too wide for the job, so for most part we used empty tins to claw out the sodden earth. We would spend days up on the hill, digging and clearing rocks from our path in treacherous conditions. Susan twisted her ankle when her foot slipped into a divot and was out of action for a week. That's when I learned that Karen had been a nurse. She did what she could, but with no doctor or medical supplies on the island, we were grateful it was nothing worse.

I would rise most mornings and join the others at the big house for breakfast. Our discussions grew longer each day, as the weather worsened and we put off heading out into the cold and wind.

There were certain subjects that we avoided talking about. Our decreasing supplies, lack of wood, Susan's near miss – anything that brought the reality of our desperate situation home. Instead we focused on what we could control, planning our days around tending to our crops, digging the new channel, fishing and trying to catch birds.

Karen and Jake grew distant. I never witnessed them argue, but every morning it seemed there was a widening gulf between them. There was a tension in the air whenever they were in the same room together. We were all aware of it, but did our best not to draw attention to it. I suspected it had something to do with Karen's brother, but thought best not to ask Jake about it. It was something they needed to figure out on their own.

Maisie was a godsend. We knew she was putting a brave face on for the kids, but her smiles and positivity had a good effect on all of us. Tom and Aillen pined occasionally for some of their old home comforts, but they felt safer on the island than they had in many months were far more adaptable to their new home than the rest of us.

As for me, I was grateful for the company. I had known isolation. Even thought I welcomed it. But now that the weather had closed in, I realised how hard it would have been trying to make it on my own.

I still ate most of my evening meals alone in my house. I needed time to think and was also conscious of giving the family some space. Afterwards, I would often receive visitors. Jake was my most frequent guest, often coming alone but sometimes with Steve in tow. With Steve around the conversation was light, peppered with his observational and self-deprecating jokes. When Jake came alone though, the conversation remained serious.

I got the feeling he didn't want to talk about the problems we faced, when his family was around. He wanted them to feel safe and optimistic, whereas with me he could be more realistic. He was a serious soul and found a match in me.

Sometimes we talked for hours, making lists of the things we needed to do to survive. We made plans for good crop yields and backup plans for bad ones. We discussed the idea of building another small catchment of water to keep fish in, when we caught more than we needed, or attempting to domesticate some of the birds.

Other times Jake said very little. We would sit on opposite sides of my small table and stare at the surface. We were I think, far more aware of our plight than the others. Or at least, we kidded ourselves that we were.

Once or twice, Karen and Maisie brought the

kids down for a visit. I would entertain them with made up stories about the previous residents of the island, who kept tigers as pets and flew around on dragons. I don't know where I got the inspiration from, but it helped to escape reality for a short time. I think Karen and Maisie enjoyed it too.

Maisie never came alone. Which was not strange at all - only Jake visited me by himself. But I found myself wishing she would. No matter how uncomfortable her presence made me. I thought about her a lot. I wondered if she remembered our fishing trip as fondly as I did. Foolish thoughts for a man stuck on an island during a nuclear winter, but thoughts they were. And I could not stop thinking them.

Maisie was the only one who persisted in asking me about my life before the island. In snatched moments, walking a distance behind the others or alone tending the crops, she would ask me questions: What did I do back in London? Was I from there originally? Where had I studied? What happened to my friends? My family? On and on it went.

But I found I didn't mind. The only part I struggled with was not being able to tell her the truth. Plus it gave me a chance to ask questions of my own.

Late one afternoon, sheltering in the big house kitchen from a particularly nasty downpour, we found ourselves alone. I decided to deflect from her usual questions by getting one of my own in first.

'So, how are you feeling about Duncan? Only, you've kept pretty quiet about the situation.'

'Yeah. It's difficult. Technically he's my brother too, but I didn't grow up with him like Karen did. We're step-sisters.'

'Ah ok. That makes sense.'

'What do you mean?'

'Well,' I felt like I'd been caught in something and needed to choose my words carefully. 'It's just that if I didn't know you and her, I never would have guessed you were sisters. You look so different.'

'Yeah I guess so. We had the same father but different mothers. Our father disappeared a long time ago. We became close when our mums passed away within a year of each other.'

I felt like an idiot for bringing it up and didn't know what to say.

'Oh… I'm sorry to hear that. Can I ask what happened?'

'Ah no it's fine, don't worry. It was a long time ago now. My mother was sick for as long as I can remember. Motor Neurone Disease. She had good years and bad, but with each one she got a little bit worse. That's the reason I stayed in the village and never really went to university. Or left Scotland actually!'

She smiled her same bulletproof smile, but there was a sadness in her eyes. I nodded but kept quiet, sensing there was more to the story.

'Karen's mum was the total opposite. One day she was fine, the next she went to the doctor with a persistent headache and was given three months at most. Brain tumor. One in a million they said.'

I shook my head. I'd had no idea and I was struck by how strong they both were.

'You've both been through so much. To have… all this happen as well. I can't imagine it. I'm so very sorry Maisie.'

'Thank you. I try to look at the positives - I got a sister out of it. Karen has her moments, but she's been good to me.'

'You're amazing, you know that? Your positivity. It's...' She was looking at me and I felt suddenly flustered and unsure of what I was saying. I felt myself blush.

'…inspiring,' I finished. 'To all of us I mean.'

She looked at me a moment longer, hard into my eyes like she was searching for something. Then she broke eye contact and stared out the window. The rain was slowing to a drizzle.

'Everybody has a story,' she said. 'I always try and remember that.'

I nodded. I knew exactly what she meant.

2

One evening, no less grey or wintery than any other, Jake arrived at my door with a plan. Although, to be fair at that moment, it wasn't so much a plan as it was a desperate idea. And it was something I'd been thinking about myself. Thinking about and rejecting, and then thinking about again. Because it wasn't just risky and foolish, but absolutely vital as well.

'I need to go back,' he said.

We were sat at my table, each with a jar of water untouched in front of us. Jake had wasted no time getting to the point.

'Karen?' I asked.

'Yeah.'

'I see.'

'I promised her I'd go back and look for him. I only said it to get her on the boat. But she won't see sense. She thinks he's still alive. Says she can feel it.'

Jake placed his elbows on the table and his

head in his hands. He didn't need to say any more. We both knew it was madness to go back to the mainland. But Karen and Jake were barely talking now and he knew if he didn't at least try, then she would never forgive him. It would hang over them forever.

A silent question hung in the air and I answered it.

'I'll come with you.'

Jake lifted his head and looked up at me. Then he shook his head.

'I can't ask you to do that.'

'You don't have to. You can't go on your own and the others have more to lose. It makes sense.'

His face was blotched red where he'd been resting it in his hands and he looked tired and worn, like an ancient rug, held together by a few remaining threads. He wanted me to come, had come specifically to ask me, but felt he couldn't. I felt a strong desire to make it easy for him.

'Besides,' I said, 'There are things we need. Wood most importantly, but if we come across any livestock, we could bring it back. Start a farm.'

He nodded.

'Thank you Carl. It'll just be a few days, I promise.'

'When do we leave?'

'Tomorrow evening before sunset. I want to arrive under cover of night and then get walking just as day breaks.'

3

Late the next day I stood alone on the shoreline staring out at the horizon. The sea was beating itself into a frenzy, like a rabid dog straining at its chain toward the man who got away.

I had not slept well the night before, my thoughts swirling around me in the dark. It is one thing to recognise a bad idea. Quite another to convince yourself to do it anyway. More than once I found myself going over another conversation in my head. One where I convinced Jake not to go through with it. I practiced what I would say to him over and over, anticipating his responses and trying to prepare for each one.

But in the cold light of morning, reality returned. I knew Jake had to go. And I could not let him go alone. If I remained, Steve or Maisie would insist on going. And if either of them didn't come back, I could not live with myself. It had to be me.

And so I stood, hands in my pockets, wind

whipping through my hair, staring out at my unknown destiny. I had barely made it once to the island, would I be so lucky the second time? And what of the dangers on the mainland?

I was so lost in my thoughts that I didn't notice Maisie approaching. She didn't look at me, just stood beside me and followed my empty gaze out to the sea.

'Nice day for it,' she said, a smile creeping up one side of her mouth.

I smiled.

'At least it's not raining,' I replied.

'...yet,' she said.

I laughed in spite of myself. As always, Maisie had a way of making me happy and anxious at the same time. Usually her presence was purposeful; she had a question or an idea she would put to me and then she would go. I was always happy to see her but relieved when she was gone. But now she just stood beside me, saying very little.

I felt the urge to say something to break the silence, but couldn't think of something that didn't sound foolish in my head. And so we stood, battered by the wind and spray from the tide, not looking at each other and not saying a word.

Finally she broke the silence. Her eyes remained facing forward.

'Come back Carl. Ok?'

I turned toward her, surprised. She looked up at me, the usual hardness missing from her eyes. I made a noise that was supposed to be a word, but came out wrong.

'Whuh?'

'I'm glad you're going with Jake. But I need you to come back.'

'I will,' I said. I hadn't meant it to sound like a promise, but that's what it was.

She placed a hand on my neck and fixed my eyes with hers for a moment. Then she glanced at my lips and leaned toward me.

'Maisie, wait,' I said.

She stepped back, the wall returning behind her eyes immediately and an edge appearing in her expression.

'No it's not what you're thinking. I want to, it's just that I have to tell you something first.'

'What?' she said. Her question said I had a second or two to answer or I would never get the opportunity to again. There was nothing left now, only the truth.

'My name isn't Carl. I'm sorry. I wanted…'

'What do you mean? What is it then?' she was angry now. I had to explain quickly but I wasn't sure how.

'I mean… my name isn't Carl. It's Vasili. Vasili Ivanov.'

She stood staring at me for a moment, mouth open. My mind raced for the next words. Something to explain myself, before she figured it out for herself.

'I wasn't involved, there was nothing I could have done, I f…' but before I could finish, something in her razor-sharp mind clicked.

'You *knew!*'

'Wait, it's not what you think!'

But she was gone and there was no more time to explain.

4

As we drifted away from the island, I stood on the aft deck watching the dock disappear into the distance. The others had headed home some time before we became a dot on the horizon, but Maisie stayed on the shore watching us leave. Just before she disappeared from view I saw her lift her hand in a half-wave, an absent minded goodbye.

I didn't wave back. My arms felt heavy, weighed down by hopelessness. Of our situation and my confession. A nuclear apocalypse had happened. Maisie knew who I was. We were headed back to a dying world on a foolhardy mission.

As far as I could tell Maisie hadn't told the others yet. But it would only be a matter of time. Even if I survived this ridiculous journey, what then? Would any of them ever speak to me again?

I didn't want to go back to the mainland. But we had no choice. We were surviving on a rocky outcrop in the middle of an icy, unforgiving ocean.

But that's all it was: surviving. Without some important supplies, it wouldn't last forever. Without a supply of wood, once winter came we would freeze. Once we became reliant on the food we could grow, one failed crop would signal the end. No, if we were going to make a go of this in the long-term, we had to go back and secure what we needed.

So we sailed on. Jake was up front steering the boat into the bleak expanse of the North Sea with a grim expression across his weary face, I was out back doing nothing more helpful than staring back towards our sanctuary as it disappeared from view.

What were we thinking? Livestock? A few chickens perhaps? Sure, great idea. But how would we capture them? How would we transport them safely back? And how would we feed them once we'd got them there?

Wood? Well that was more practical and it was the one resource we needed more than anything else at that moment. We had plenty of canned goods to keep us going and the right tools between us to fish and maintain our homes. But we didn't have the material we needed to make repairs and build fires. There would be plenty of trees to chop down, but we'd have to find the right tools first and it would be heavy work for the two of us. Could we hope to chop down and lug back enough to last us through the winter? Jake had an idea of planting pine trees on the island. And it was a good one, but it would still be a few years before we could make use of them.

These concerns were on both of our minds, but went unspoken as we continued our slow and steady progression south. It was the elephant of despair in our floating, rocking room.

Of course, neither the wood nor the animals, were the 'official' reason for the trip - officially, at least to Karen anyway, we were headed back to rescue Duncan. Any supplies we could bring back with us would just be a bonus to the real mission. And perhaps finding Duncan was the most hopeless goal of all. He was a needle we were supposed to find amid a burning haystack.

If Duncan had survived, had somehow managed to escape the gang and then found a way to live out in the wilderness, how on earth were we to find him? The world was a dangerous place now - it wasn't like we could casually drive from village to village asking if anyone had seen him.

I knew Jake was thinking this. But he must also have been worrying about what the alternative was - returning without him. Would Karen accept that he was gone, morn and move on? Or would she think Jake hadn't looked hard enough, or worse, blame him for Duncan's demise. Either way, I didn't envy him.

A yawn caught me by surprise, so wide it strained my jaw and made my eyes water. I was exhausted. Not just from lack of sleep the night before, but from everything that we'd been through and everything we had to come. The very thought of it made me want to lie down and sleep for the rest of time. No more surviving against a backdrop of death and destruction. No more fear of the sinister elements of society. No more worrying about this most uncertain of futures. Just the peace and tranquility of an endless sleep.

5

When Maisie finally returned to the house, Karen thought she detected a frosty demeanor around her. Instead of joining the rest of the family in the front room, she walked through the hall to the kitchen and right out the back door, grabbing a shovel on the way.

Karen wasn't confused by this. Not exactly. She hadn't expected it, that was all. She wasn't angry with Maisie either. She knew that the rest of the family thought she was being stupid, demanding that Jake go back and look for Duncan. Maisie was just the only one who would dare to show it, even if only in the subtlest of ways. She didn't expect Maisie to understand though, or any of the others for that matter. She knew Duncan was still alive. She *knew*. There had never been a doubt in her mind and she was sure that if anything had happened to him, she would have had one. Or felt… something anyway.

She knew that Maisie and I had become close. She wasn't sure if the others had noticed it, certainly not the men, but she had. Maisie had been careful not to be seen to show any favour towards me in front of them. But she'd seen the stolen glances made towards each other, when the other was looking away. And anyway, she'd always had a radar for these sorts of things.

Perhaps that's why Maisie was giving her the cold shoulder. Maybe it wasn't directed at her at all - maybe she was upset that I had gone with Jake and just didn't want anyone to notice.

Either way, she would leave Maisie to herself for a while and let her cool off. Everything would be ok, she'd see.

6

Though the consequences would be grave for all of us, I bear Karen no ill will for what she did.

We can only imagine the guilt she must have felt. She had found a safe corner to hide from a burning world, while her brother was lost in the furnace. And it was his idea, his safe corner. This was no ordinary situation for her or any of us. She was no longer a normal working mother, resigned to the drudgery of everyday life. She was now a survivor, living life day to day, fearing for her children's future and missing her brother who she felt she had left behind for her own safety.

As Jake and I sailed on through the dark night and rough seas on our way back to the mainland, Karen rose early one last time, to give her plan one last go.

She settled herself onto the uncomfortable wooden chair in the cramped, cold radio room. Every week for several months now, she had done the same thing, her heart filled with hope, her mind filled with despair. She expected that night to be no different.

She had resolved herself to make this one final attempt. To reach out and try to contact somebody, somewhere, who may be able to help Jake and I locate Duncan. Or at the very least, to find out that the worst had happened. But she didn't believe it had. *Couldn't* believe it had. He was Duncan, her sometimes silly, sometimes stubborn and occasionally exceptionally frustrating brother. She couldn't imagine never seeing him again.

So she turned the dials one last time, repeating her message through the wall of static.

"My name is Karen. I am with my family on a small island to the north of Scotland. I am trying to reach my brother Duncan, who was last seen on the mainland. If anyone can hear me, please respond."

Once again, even with the volume on the lowest setting, she was overwhelmed by the sound of the white noise coming from the radio. It felt too loud on an island where the only other sounds were the howl of the wind and the crash of the waves against the harsh rocks.

"My name is Karen. I am with my family on a small island to the north of Scotland. I am trying to reach my brother Duncan, who was last seen on the mainland. If anyone can hear me, please respond."

Nothing. Nothing and nothing but static.

She carried out her routine nonetheless, turning the tuning dial slowly through the band, repeating her message intermittently. Every time she pressed the button to speak the static would cut out. She would wait two minutes for a reply, counting off the seconds in her head, before shifting the dial a notch and trying again.

Margins of success are so very small in life that we barely notice them. A missed train that leads to a chance encounter. A broken umbrella in the rain that inexplicably leads to a new job. In everything we do there are an overwhelming number of opportunities which we are blinded to by the monotony of our everyday lives. On a base level we are aware of this, but instead of treating it as a ray of hope in the grind of routine, we let it force us into more negative habits. One last check of the emails before we sleep. Perhaps once more in the dead of night. Just in case. We don't seem to understand that opportunities come from putting ourselves out there, not from doing the same mundane and pointless things over and over again.

Which is not of course, to be confused with perseverance. Perseverance for a personal cause is far more difficult then loading up the instagram feed just one more time. Perseverance means facing failure again and again in pursuit of something meaningful to us. We are tired, desperate, broken. But we give it one more go anyway. For ambition, for love, for a dream of a better life. Not to make sure we see the very latest picture of someone else's perfect holiday.

And it was perseverance to find her brother that led Karen to do what she did that night. She went through the entire width of the dial the same as she always did. Once to the top and then back to the beginning. With the same results as before.

On any other night that is where she would have stopped. She would have turned off the radio and crept back to the house, in fear of being discovered as she always was. But this night was different. Whether it was because Jake and I were headed back to the island, whether it was because she had decided that this would be the last time she crept out to the radio in the dead of night, or whether it was just *because*, she decided to give it one more go.

Small margins.

Mid-way up the band, just as she reached 120 seconds in her head and lifted her arm towards the dial, there was a crackle she hadn't heard before. It came and went in a flash, but it was unmistakably different from the snap and hiss she had heard before.

She waited, breath held, heart beating hard against her chest. She tried to still it, worried that the sound of her own blood ringing in her ears would make her miss the sound again.

There it was again! She repeated her message and sat up in her chair, on high alert.

The crackle came again. And then again. An unpleasant scratch through the wall of white noise.

An idea struck her. She repeated her message but this time ended it with the frequency through which she was broadcasting. Or at least, her best guess of it. The numbers around the dial were well worn and only the minimum and maximum could be made out. She was somewhere in the middle, so could only guess.

Another crackle louder and longer this time. It

shifted in pitch and volume, lurching back and forth through the hiss. And then suddenly there it was, a voice through the haze.

'…hear me? Hello? Is somebody…hear… there?'

It was a man's voice, deep and thick with a Glaswegian accent.

Urgently, but ever so carefully, she tweaked the dial, raising her voice as she called out to him, her fear of being caught temporarily forgotten.

'Hello? Yes I can hear you! My name is Karen, can you hear me? You're breaking up. Please keep trying!'

Finally, after several minutes of tweaking and trying, the static reduced to a low buzz and the man's voice was clear enough to be heard.

'…think it's a woman. Shut-up will you Greig, I'm trying to listen'

'Hello!' she almost shouted, 'I can hear you! You're coming through loud and clear! Can you hear me ok?'

'That's it, don't touch the flaming dial, we've got her! Hello…Karen is it? Did I hear that right?' the man said.

'Yes! Who are you? *Where* are you?'

'My name is…Callum. We've been trying to reach someone with this old radio for sometime, hoping for any news. Where are you radioing from?'

In her enthusiasm, she missed that he hadn't answered her question.

'I'm… we're on an island to the north of the mainland. St. Rita. We're ok. I'm trying to reach my brother Duncan. Do you have contact with anyone near Drumbeg? That's where we last saw him. We had to leave in a hurry and he didn't… make the boat.'

She was babbling and she knew it, her excitement uncontrollable. She tried to give the man time to respond.

'Drumbeg yes! We're not far from there Karen, not far at all.'

Hope soared in her chest. Of course, she never considered the fact that the old radio may not have had a long range and may only have been useful to contact passing ships in times of emergency. She just felt incredibly lucky and filled with a desperate urge to find out what she could, in case the signal was lost and the voice on the other end gone forever.

She ploughed on.

'Do you know a Duncan? Duncan is his name. He's my brother. He's from Drumbeg. Have you heard of him at all?'

'Greig, do we know a Duncan?' he was talking to another man. She thought she could hear a smile on his lips, but noticed it only in passing and thought nothing of it. If his question received a reply, she didn't hear. It. There was a pause and she wondered - *hoped,* that they were discussing it and trying to remember. Finally the voice returned.

'Karen, we think we might know of a Duncan, but we can't be sure. We'll try and get a message out to the surrounding villages. But we'll need to confirm he's the right person. Wouldn't want to get your hopes up for no good reason. Can you tell us more about you and your… friends? Particularly the island and how you came to be there? It might help us locate him and be sure, you understand?'

Karen hesitated. Although it seemed like a reasonable request, she remembered all too well the reasons she had fled to the island. And the people she had fled from. There would be nowhere else to escape to if they found her and her family again.

'Karen? Are you there?' the voice crackled through her thoughts and flustered her. Waves of white noise had started to intrude on the connection. Aware that she could lose the signal at any moment, she decided she had to take a chance. The guilt of leaving her brother behind was eating at her every day - far worse a punishment (she thought) than anything anyone else could do to her.

'Yes. Yes of course,' she said. 'Whatever you think might help.'

And then she told them. About her escape from the mainland. About our island. Everything they needed to know.

7

The North Atlantic Ocean is always rough. It rises and batters and collapses in on itself, never ceasing for a moment, lest the world think that it is not angry. Our boat, which felt large to me when we left the shore, but now felt very little, chugged its way over the peaks and troughs through the night. Jake and I were alone, with nothing but the angry sea for company.

We had been sailing for several hours now, without uttering a single word to each other. The salty spray had dampened our clothes, dried our skin and reddened our eyes. But still we ploughed on, to a destination neither of us wanted to reach.

I wondered if Jake had considered turning back as many times as I had. When humans are faced with something we don't want to do, our animal brains are very good at convincing us to avoid it. Call it a primal defense mechanism, if you will. It's probably the reason so many people don't turn up for job interviews, despite toiling through the application process and calling to confirm the day before. A job interview is the great unknown. And our human brains do not like the unknown.

'Turn back,' they say. 'You don't *have* to do this. You could just go home and maybe do it again some other day.'

Even though I knew we must press on, still my mind tried to convince me to turn back. 'You don't need to do this *today*,' it said. 'Perhaps come back after a few more weeks when things have settled down a bit more on the mainland,'

Given that I had nothing to do but battle with my own mind, I began to marvel at this quirk of biological engineering. I understood *why* our minds behaved this way; they were designed to keep us safe. Change was not safe. It could not be controlled. That's the reason that, much like other animals, humans crave routine on a subconscious level. But when it was something we *knew* we had to do, why then did our defense mechanism kick in this way? It was just another hurdle to climb over.

Therein lies the human conundrum. We often *decide* that we must do something (or stop doing something), we *know* this to be true in our hearts and in our minds. Yet the brain still treats this thing as something to be avoided. As something it must do it's best to riddle it's way out of. Our own brains try to trick us into taking an easier path. So the question is, who's really in control here?

A hard crash at the bottom of a trough brought me sharply up from my philosophical musing with a crash and a spray of ice cold salt water. I rubbed my eyes to clear the salt. Which only served to make them sting more.

Jake was in the middle of the boat, at the wheel of the pleasure craft. Although there was a comfortable leather seat to sit in, he was standing. He had been the entire trip so far. I decided to offer to take over. Anything to take my mind away from it's endless cycle of internal conflict.

'Jake,' I said. Then once again, when he didn't hear me. He looked locked in a grim trance, jaw tight and mouth pulled down to one side. I raised my hand and placed it gently on his shoulder, the polite tap of a man in a crowded bar, making his way to the gents.

He turned slightly to face me, his expression unchanged. There was a question in his eyes.

'Do you want me to take over for a bit?' There was more to say: *It doesn't look too complicated* or *I think I can keep us on the right compass heading for a while*, but neither of those questions came out. We were both so distracted by our own thoughts and fears that extraneous words were beyond us.

He shook his head, no, and then returned to looking dead-ahead.

I felt something had developed between Jake and I over the short time we'd known each other. A level of trust and respect that was not quite friendship, but was in the current circumstance, much more important. I got the impression that we alone knew the true peril we faced, trying to survive on the island. It was a false impression of course, all of us were more than aware, but it was one that we shared. And it had forged a bond between us.

I moved back to my place at the back of the boat and grasped the cold wet steel of the rifle as I sat down. I looked at the gun in my hand and wondered who I was now. The old me of some months ago felt a very long way away. I cannot say whether I longed for him to return or not.

Staring at the gun, I wondered again for the first time in months, if I would have to use it. Bringing it had been an obvious choice. If I hadn't, I'm sure Jake would have. Or failing that, Maisie would have insisted.

I doubt any of us would have thought for a second, that it would have been more useful left back on the island.

8

Shortly before the sun threatened to rise the next day, in the sweeping grey of pre-dawn, Jake finally spoke. It was just a single word.

'Carl'.

I didn't respond at first. It took a small hesitation before I realised he was speaking to me. I reminded myself that I was Carl and hurried over to him, lest he notice my delay and not mistake it for being in a trance made of boredom and anxiety.

'Land-ho,' he nodded in the direction of the bow There was no hint of exuberance in his voice.

I strained my eyes against the poor light. And there it was. The unmistakable silhouette of land, standing in front of us like a crumbling wall that stretched the length of the horizon. My heart jumped back up from where it had slipped down to over the course of the long journey, to take its place again in my throat. *Now* we were nearly there. *Now* it was real.

'I'm not going to risk the port,' he said. I know

an isolated spot further down. It's a farther walk to… civilisation,' he couldn't find a better word for it, 'But the boat should be safe there,'

I said nothing in response. There was no need to. Jake and Steve had been sailing around this northern coast line for several years, in this very same boat. I had only been here once - the night of my escape from a nuclear apocalypse in a dingy not made for the journey.

Jake killed the engine to a low growl as we drew within a mile. Whether this was a natural thing to do, or whether it was a desire to not be heard, I can't be certain. But either way, both our eyes stayed fixed on the mainland. There was no sign of life.

After cruising slowly for a short while, a small rocky beach came into view, with what looked like a black, sanded spot to one side.

'I'm going to anchor her Carl,' he said. 'I'll need you to jump off quick and tie her up. There's a rocky outcrop just a few metres up from the shore. Wrap a couple of loops round and tie her tight. Then come back and get the second rope from the starboard side and find another rock at least five metres from the first. I'll need to keep the engine going until we're anchored good and strong. There's a lot of sharp rocks in the bay and we can't afford to drift on to one of them.'

'Understood,' I said.

Jumping off the front of the boat, the icy water rose to my knees and shocked me back to full alert. My heart thumped hard in my chest as I raced up the damp sand, falling once as my foot sunk in, before getting to the outcrop and pulling the rope around as tight as I could.

Once I got the second rope done, Jake leased the anchor and killed the engine. He jumped off the deck and came to stand by me, handing me the rifle. We stood staring back at the boat for a short while, neither of us in a hurry to move on with the next step.

Finally, Jake said 'She'll hold,' and we turned and made our way slowly up the rocky shore to the top of the small cliff.

9

Jake and I crested the top of the hill that led down towards the cliff and looked around us.

Fifty metres or so ahead was a single-lane track, asphalt, but with no road markings. Off to our right the track followed the coastline, but after a short distance to the left, it headed inland. Beyond it, there was nothing but rocky headland.

'So, what's the plan?' I asked.

Jake thought for a minute. 'Well, I think we need to make our way towards my old village and scope it out. But as to how we get there, there's two options. Both of which will take a fair bit of walking.'

'I thought you might say that,' I said, with a small smile. Jake was surprised by my attempt at humour, but attempted a smile of his own. It came out more like a grimace. I wondered when the last time he'd managed one was.

'The first option is to follow the road. It'll be easier walking... but we'll be easier to spot.' Both of us had spent so long avoiding talking about what might happen when we got here, that it was proving hard to shake off. 'The second option would be to stay off road. I'm pretty sure I can get us there without it, but the walking will be harder'.

There was a short silence. Both of us knew which option we were going to take, but neither of us wanted to say it, for fear of acknowledging out-loud the danger we might be in.

I broke the silence. 'We should probably remain unseen for as long as we can,' I said.

Jake nodded. We crossed the road and continued on, into the damp, uneven grass.

After two hours of traipsing through the rough, rocky wildland, our boots were soaked and it had begun to drizzle. There was a weak but persistent wind blowing in from the coast and we were cold, wet and anxious as ever. Both of us had taken our fair share of tumbles, our feet slipping into unseen divots or catching against a hidden rock. Progress was miserable and slow.

Although we'd stayed far enough away from the road not to be spotted, we would still have heard an engine, if so much as a small car had gone past. But we'd heard nothing at all, save for the sound of our grunts as we trudged through the uneven ground. So when we saw the first signs of civilisation, it came as a shock.

We ascended a small rise to look down on a farmhouse some half-a-mile away, surrounded by nothing but fields apart from a large barn standing to the left of it. We stood staring down at the farm, breath held. But there was no movement below and no one to be seen. Eventually Jake suggested we take a look and if it felt abandoned, see if there was anything worth salvaging. Maybe rest up for a bit. I agreed.

As we made our way down I realised I was clenching the rifle hard against my chest. I tried to relax my grip, telling myself that even if we did come upon someone, there was no guarantee they would be hostile towards us. And pointing the gun at them probably wouldn't help.

When we got to the near wall of the farmhouse we sat at the base, backs against the wall, listening for any sound. There was nothing but the wind. I was the one with the weapon, so indicated that I would go first. Jake looked uncertain, but nodded his agreement.

I held the gun downwards, pointed at the ground but ready to pull it up in a heartbeat. I rounded the wall at a slight crouch and stared at the front door. Still no signs of anyone. I waived for Jake to follow and then made my way slowly toward the entrance to the house. There were two small steps up to the door, which was painted white but had faded to near gray over many years. There were six small square windows at the top of it, in two rows of three. I crept up the steps and stood just tall enough to peer through the lower row.

Inside the house was dark and I could only make out a hallway with stairs going upwards on the right wall. I couldn't see anything else. I crouched back down on the doorstep and motioned for Jake to approach. When he got to me I whispered in the lowest voice I could, which still sounded too loud to my own ears.

'I can't see much. There's a hallway and some stairs but no other windows so it's too dark.'

'Let me look,' Jake replied.

We swapped places and Jake peered through the windows. He remained that way for a while and then raised his hand to the door knob and as quietly as possible, tested it. The door was locked. He rejoined me and both of us crouched against the wall, right next to the door.

'You keep an eye out,' Jake whispered. 'I'll check around back.'

As he snuck around the far side of the house, I scanned the area once again. It looked like any old farmhouse you might see in Britain. A mix of tire tracks and mud around the buildings, gradually fading into patches of green in the distance. The fields in the surrounding area were organised by hedge rows of varying symmetry.

I couldn't see any vehicles or animals and I had to wonder if the previous inhabitants had abandoned the place some time ago. Perhaps even before the catastrophe. There just wasn't anything to suggest that anybody had been there recently.

I looked at the barn. Perhaps that would solve one of our immediate problems - we could take it apart for wood. That felt like a big job for the two of us though, especially without a vehicle to lug it back to the boat.

Jake was back. I noticed that he was standing straighter and guessed that he had found nothing to suggest that we weren't still alone.

'You need to see this,' he said.

I followed him, with a sinking feeling. There was something in his expression that suggested my *need* to see whatever it was, would not be the same as me *wanting* to. And I was right.

Although Jake hadn't found a way in, the rear of the house had a pair of full window patio doors, which opened onto a small decking area. These doors were also locked, but gave access to the grim scene inside the house.

The body of a man lay face down, splayed out in front of a large armchair. From the angle of the body, it looked as though he'd fallen forward out of the armchair and died in that very position. We could tell he was dead because of the state of his skin and flesh. It looked as though he'd been there for a while.

'There's no sign of struggle in the room,' I said, voice now raised above a whisper. 'Maybe he died of natural causes. Or maybe of…'

'...something else.' Jake finished the thought for me.

As we stood staring through the window, a light rain began to fall, like a prelude to the rolling storm of our dawning comprehension.

10

Maisie awoke early, with an unsteady feeling in the pit of her stomach. Something wasn't right.

She sat up in her bed and stared out the window as she stretched and tried to rub the aches out of her back. It was no use though. After months spent sleeping on the camping bed, she had grown used to it, but her back had not.

It was just after dawn outside but the sun showed little sign of its presence. The sky was dull, grey and overcast with a threat of the kind of light drizzle that falls all day, not enough to soak you, but enough so that any time spent outdoors soon became unpleasant.

She listened for a moment, but the only sounds she could hear were the ever present waves crashing against the shore. She tried to shake off her feeling of unease. *It's probably just the boys being gone*, she thought. *There's nothing to be done about it. I'll feel better once they're back.*

She rose slowly and carefully, trying not to make too much noise and wake the others. She was usually the first one up in the big house and despite the isolation of the island, still valued those first few moments of the day that she had to herself. She pulled on a hoodie over her sleeping clothes and made her way downstairs.

When she arrived at the doorway to the kitchen she froze. Karen was there, standing by the window, a cup of something warm in her hands.

'Oh! Sorry Maisie, I didn't mean to scare you,' she said.

Maisie composed herself and entered the kitchen. Pouring herself some water and settling onto a chair.

'How long have you been up?' she asked.

'Oh, most of the night,' said Karen. And then her eyes went wide and she corrected herself, 'Well, on and off, you know'.

Maisie was confused. She felt like Karen was keeping something from her, but she didn't push it.

'I can't stop thinking about Carl and Jake,' she said, wishing she had said Jake's name first as soon as the words were out of her mouth.

'No neither can I. I'm sure they'll be back soon though and everything will be back to… well not normal, but whatever *this* is.'

It was unlike Karen to be the optimistic one and this fact was not missed by Maisie. But again, she didn't want to push it. She thought they must all be feeling a little off at the moment, what with the uncertainty of the trip.

Maisie changed the subject. 'Looks like it's not going to be much fun out there today,' she said, nodding towards the window.

'Unlike every other day,' Karen said, with a chuckle. Now Maisie couldn't ignore it. There was definitely something going on. Karen hadn't made a single joke since they'd arrived on the island.

'Karen, what's going on?' she said, a little bit more forcefully than she'd intended.

'Nothing,' she said, after a slight hesitation. 'What do you mean?'

'I've known you a long time Karen. I can tell when something's not right. And right now it sure feels like something isn't right'.

Karen sighed. Maisie thought she could see the cogs turning behind her eyes.

'No it's nothing Maisie, I swear. I think I'm just a mixture of scared and excited you know? About Jake and Carl being away. And well, about them bringing Duncan back. I know he's alive Maisie. I *know* it.'

It was a reasonable excuse, given the circumstances. But there was something about the way Karen had said she *knew* Duncan was alive that put Maisie on edge. Karen had been saying that very same thing every day since they'd arrived. Often when arguing with Jake. But this time it sounded somehow *stronger*. She wasn't sure if it was delusion or… something else. But whatever it was, it only served to make the uneasy feeling in her chest that much worse.

11

It is common for humans to think they are the centre of all things. That the rotation of the earth, the sun and all the galaxies of the universe, exist just for us. Though our rational mind may know different, deep in our subconscious we *feel* we are both the cause and the reason for the being of everything. As we traverse our short lives, becoming embroiled in the current passions of the day, we forget that we are completely inconsequential to the vastness of time and space. Our planet will continue to turn, with or without us and our petty squabbles.

As Jake and I trudged through a field of dead sheep, this realisation crept up on our weary minds. We were coming to understand that our greatest threat was not from man (or at least, a group of bad men) but rather from the hell that humanity had unleashed on itself. A threat not just to us, but to all living things on earth.

'How much further?' I asked, wiping my damp forehead with an even more wet forearm.

Jake stopped and looked up at the horizon. We were at the far end of a seemingly endless series of muddy fields. We had struggled through each one, the ground beneath our feet growing increasingly soft and sludgy as the rain grew harder.

The sky ahead was a mixture of greys, overcast to the point where we couldn't be sure where the sun was. There was a fence a few hundred metres ahead, barely visible against the uneven hills and shrouded in brown and dark green. However, just beyond the fence was what looked like a thin strip of asphalt, heading around the corner to the left.

I had been labouring under the assumption that Jake knew exactly where we were going, but as he stood there, eyes scanning from left to right and brow furrowed, I wasn't so sure. Finally his eyes seemed to rest on a point to the far left, where the road disappeared.

'I'm not sure,' he said. 'But I think that road leads to a junction with a B-road, which if I'm right, will take us to Drumbeg.

I paused, waiting to see if there was more, but he appeared to be finished.

'Is that where Duncan would be?' I asked.

Jake shook his head. 'No. But I know people in that village who know him and might know where he is.'

He didn't sound very confident and I could tell he was distracted. Since seeing the dead man alone in his living room, we had continued on without saying a word to each other, each of us lost in the implications of what we had seen. Even while passing the sorry sight of the dead flock, laying like rotting pillows around us, we had trudged on in silence. The evidence was all around us in that field. There was no need to reinforce our dark thoughts with any darker conversation.

Jake glanced at me and I nodded. We set off again.

12

As Jake and I trudged on, back on the ocean a large grey vessel, which was currently about halfway between the mainland and our island, sailed northward. Black smoke chugged from the engine, matching the colour of the makeshift flag that hung from the back of it on a thin metal pole. It looked like the boat of death itself.

Onboard, a thick-set man lay on an uncomfortable bunk in a small, damp cabin, coughing uncontrollably. A tattooed hand patted his shoulder and he settled.

'Won't be long now Ian. There's a nurse on the island and it should be far enough north for the air to be clear of any radiation. You'll be right as rain in no time.'

The sick man groaned in acknowledgement.

13

After making it to the edge of the last field and climbing the fence, Jake and I hugged the small track and found it much easier going. The rain had steadied and was just on the border between a moderate shower and a driving pelt. It was just light enough for us to keep going, but not light enough to avoid causing us constant discomfort. We were soaked through now and splattered with mud and dirt up to our knees. Time now though, was everything. And so we pressed on.

We paused at the arrival of a T-junction. Our small road had come to an end as it met a much bigger one steaming across its path. This road was dual-laned and had painted markings. A proper road. A *main* road.

'What do you think?' Jake asked. He didn't have to say about what.

I considered for a moment as I swept my head left to right and listened hard against the rain for any sound of a vehicle.

Up until we clambered out of the last field, we'd avoided coming into close proximity with a road like this, or any other which might have allowed us to be spotted by a passing vehicle. But since our encounter at the farmhouse and uninterrupted trek along the track, our thinking had altered somewhat. Not enough to avoid giving us pause at this main thoroughfare however.

'Let's cross over and stay close to that hedgerow. We can always dive for cover if we hear anything coming,' I said.

Jake nodded.

'Which way are we heading?' I asked him.

'Down that way,' he said, pointing off to the left where the road continued on towards a gap between two sizable hills.

In spite of ourselves and our situation, we both looked left and right before crossing. Old habits die hard I guess.

We continued along the side of the road for more than an hour. More than once one of us grabbed the other and hurtled for the brambles a few feet from the road. After several minutes of sitting in the ditch, scratched from head to toe and breathing hard, we would agree that whatever sound we'd perceived was nothing and pull ourselves back out to continue on.

After going through this uncomfortable routine multiple times, we grew more hesitant and would stop and listen hard for a moment, rather than dive headlong into the thorns. It wasn't complacency, more just a growing confidence (and a growing unease) that nothing and nobody was travelling this road but us.

The clouds grew ever darker and the rain began to hammer us into a stoop, our heads bent downwards and arms raised regularly to shield our faces from the onslaught. Finally, we caught sight of a sign up ahead.

"Welcome to Drumbeg. Please mind your speed."

There was another smaller sign below it, a red ring around a white circle with bold black numbers indicating a maximum speed of thirty miles per hour. I wondered when the last time was that a car had passed that sign, slowing as the driver pressed lightly on the brake.

This sudden, familiar scene of civilisation, halted me in my tracks. I felt at once both comforted by what it resembled and distraught at its loss.

'Carl,' Jake's voice was firm but had an undercurrent of panic beneath it.

My mind snapped out of reflection and I realised Jake had also come to a halt, just a few paces ahead of me. He was stood stock upright, his body like a spring stretched to its limit, ready to recoil the second it was released.

As I joined him, I noticed that he was staring hard at something in the distance. I shielded my eyes with my right hand and strained my vision against the rain and failing light.

At first it was hard to see what had caught his attention, but as my eyes adjusted to a longer focus, I could make out a small dwelling some distance on from the sign. It had off-white walls punctuated by small dark windows and covered in an old-fashioned thatched roof, which looked like it had seen better times. I was focusing hard at one of the windows, trying to determine if there was the flickering of a light inside, when a slow movement caught my eye over by the door. This was what Jake had noticed and was the reason he had stayed stock still and called me, rather than crouching or diving for cover.

There was a man standing on the doorstep. His left hand was raised over his eyes. He held something long and sharp in his right hand. And he was staring right back at us.

14

The man made his move first.

We had stood there for a long moment, past the point of denial for either party over what they were seeing. My hand had crept involuntarily back to the hilt of the rifle, which was slung over my shoulder. The feel of the hard, wet wood was reassuring, but I was anxious over whether I could ready it in time if I needed to.

Jake must have sensed my movement next to him and spoke under his breath: 'Not yet.'

Neither of us could tell what the long tool the stranger held in his hand was, but as he began to take hesitant steps towards us it became obvious that it was some sort of walking aid. The thought didn't relax me however. Guns could make fine walking sticks too.

The man continued coming towards us, his pace slowed by more than just his limp. He was hesitant too. And that did provide some comfort to me.

When he reached the sign he stopped, as though the boundary provided the limit within which he felt safe. He was still too far away for us to make out his features. He paused for a moment, before raising his free hand in slow wave and calling out to us.

'Hullo there!' It was almost a question.

At the sound of his voice, carrying towards us over the sound of the pounding rain, I felt Jake relax next to me. He exhaled hard, several moments of breath held and now released.

'I think I know him,' he said. And then louder, towards the man, 'Jimmy? Is that you? It's Jake. Jake Mitchell!'

The man limped forward another pace or two, breaking the invisible border between us.

'Jakey? As I live and breathe! We thought you were dead!'

Jake placed a hand on my shoulder, 'We're ok, I know him.' he repeated. He looked at me, reassurance in his eyes and an unspoken request for trust. I released my hand from the rifle and he nodded.

Jake began walking towards Jimmy and I followed just behind, my eyes scanning hard for any other movement.

As we drew close the man smiled.

'Jakey boy! It is you!' He covered the few remaining paces between us and slung his arms around Jake. Jake returned the hug but I could tell he was still hesitant with his old acquaintance.

Much like the roof of his house, I could see that Jimmy had also seen better days. His skin was pale and blotchy and had begun to flake on his forehead. He looked weak and old, leaning hard on his walking stick, but his face was not that of an older man. He looked to be no more than 45.

He released Jake and placed his free hand on his shoulder, gripping it hard, his knuckles turning white.

'It's good to see you Jake. And looking so well. We had heard the Pirates were on your trail and feared the worst.'

The way he kept using the word 'we' made me nervous. I couldn't see signs of anyone else around us, nor any movement from the house. If Jimmy had a partner or was part of a group, where were they?

'It's good to see you to Jimmy,' Jake was giving nothing away. 'But what are you doing down here?'

The question implied that this was not where Jimmy's lived. Another thought which disturbed me. I fought hard against the desire to reach back again for my rifle.

'Ach… it's a long story Jake. Let's get inside and I'll explain. There's no power, but at least we'll be out of this muck.' he said, referring to the downpour.

He turned and nodded for us to follow. Jake paused a beat and then followed. And I followed him.

15

Inside, the house was dark and a bit of a mess. There were broken and unwashed dishes left in small piles everywhere and dirt and grit all over the stained carpet.

Jimmy led us towards the back and into what must have been the living room of the old house. This room was in an even worse state, with discarded clothing joining the piles of plates, mugs and glasses. But at least a large double window at the back allowed some decent light in.

There was an old fashioned three piece suite, faded green with threadbare tassels hanging around the fringes. Jimmy collapsed onto the end of the two seater sofa, leaving the two dusty armchairs for us. He motioned for us to sit.

It was there in the dimly lit living room of an old house in the north western reaches of Scotland, where the full realisation of what had happened on the mainland hit home. Staring at Jimmy, his frame thin, his skin peeling, his eyes bloodshot and his movements racked with pain, it was undeniable.

Jake couldn't hold back his questions.

'What happened to you Jimmy? Where's Margaret? And the girls?'

Jimmy gave Jake a confused look.

'Where've you been Jake? Do you not know what's happened?'

Jake deflected the question again.

'We've kept ourselves as far away as possible. Because of the Pirates you see,' he was thinking on his feet.

'But have none of you got sick?' Jimmy asked, an urgency and disbelief in his voice.

Jake didn't have time to consider his response before Jimmy asked another question.

'And who's your comrade here?' he motioned toward me with a limp hand, 'I've not seen him before.'

Comrade. The word made me wince. Had it just been a turn of phrase or had he seen something in my face? In my features? Would it give Jake pause for thought? If it did, he didn't show it. He jumped at the chance to steer the question away from where we'd been hiding.

'This is Carl, Jimmy. An old friend of mine from a long while ago. We met on the road some months back, both of us on the run from the Pirates. But what about Margaret? Where is she?' he asked again.

Jimmy sighed. He looked up at the ceiling and

breathed in hard and laboured. I could tell he was holding back a tear.

'Jimmy?' Jake asked again, his voice softer this time.

Jimmy exhaled hard and fixed his focus on the dirty carpet.

'She's gone. They're all gone. What have we done Jimmy-boy?' and then again, almost to himself, 'What have we done?'

The room filled with silence, like a thick black tar being poured into a gaping hole. It was broken seconds later by a flash of hot white light and a booming thunder clap, which seemed to vibrate the very walls around us.

16

That night I lay awake in one of the bedrooms of the small home, staring into the impenetrable dark at a ceiling I knew was there, but couldn't see.

I kept going over and over Jimmy's sad story in my head. At first they had just been living in fear of food shortages and the Pirates. But then people had started arriving from the south. Just a trickle to begin with, but then more and more. Refugees that had survived the explosions and the immediate fall of society afterwards. A desperate migration north in the hope of avoiding the radiation sickness that had taken their friends, family members and neighbours.

Most of them were already showing the signs of illness when they arrived. They paused once they reached Drumbeg and the surrounding villages, as the inhabitants did not appear to have been radiated. At least on the surface.

Along with those desperate for safety from a threat that no wall could restrain, were those few whose darker nature had been allowed to flourish by the new lawlessness. But their numbers too, were weakening. While food and power had been their number one driver, now health was. Their focus switched from warring with each other to enabling anyone with any medical or scientific training to help them. Rough medical centres had been set up and they worked together to secure any medicines and equipment the doctors needed. But it was all to no avail.

Radioactive ash had fallen all over the mainland, polluting the fields that the animals grazed in and the rivers and lakes that people had turned to once the water had been shut off.

One by one, people grew sick. Some very fast, others more slowly, with no more than a persistent cough that wouldn't go away. That was when people began moving on again. Well, those that were healthy enough to anyway.

Jimmy didn't know where they had gone, he assumed further North, perhaps to the far North Eastern reaches of Scotland or maybe even on boats to the Shetland Isles. All he knew is that they never returned and the village was mostly deserted now.

He had been healthy enough to go, but his wife and two daughters were bed-ridden and he couldn't leave them. His younger daughter passed first, followed by his oldest and then after another couple of months, his wife. Although he had nowhere else to go, Jimmy couldn't stay in the house where he'd raised his family anymore. It was all too painful and he had grown too sick to even to bury his wife.

He knew that the owners of the cottage on the edge of the village had fled north and so he moved down there to die. He thought he had just enough food and water to last him until the end. Not that he could eat much anymore. Instead he had taken to drinking whatever alcohol he could find, to numb his nerves and any feelings he had left.

Jake and I had been the first people he'd seen in a long while.

Although I knew Jake wanted desperately to ask if Jimmy had heard or seen anything about Duncan, he held back. Jimmy's story was too shocking and painful to be passed over quickly. He was so spent after telling it, racked with tears and a persistent cough, that he simply lay back on the couch, his vacant stare fixed at the ceiling. He made to indicate that we could stay, but a violent shaking took over him and Jake just placed a hand on his shoulder, told him to rest and that we would talk in the morning. By the end of Jimmy's story the day was over anyway, the little light there was fading rapidly.

I cannot tell you the tangled mix of thoughts and emotions which coiled around me and gripped at my chest that night. Sympathy for Jimmy, horror at what had befallen the world, relief that we had survived the radiation, fear that it was only a matter of time before we were radiated and a gnawing, desperate urge to get back to the island as fast as possible.

I didn't know what Jake was thinking, but I could imagine it was the same. I knew he wouldn't want to leave without finding Duncan, or at least, finding out what had happened to him. But the longer we were exposed to that environment, the more chance we would face irreparable damage. I hoped Jake wouldn't take too long to decide what to do.

17

Maisie woke hard and fast, sitting bolt upright in the darkness of the pre-dawn morning. A loud noise had torn her from her slumber, but she couldn't place it. She sat trying to control her breathing and listening to hear it again.

At first there was nothing, just the sound of the wind and the waves whipping the shoreline. The storm, which had been threatening an assault all throughout the previous day, had finally been released. She relaxed a little, thinking that perhaps it had just been a large thunder clap or wave hitting the rocks that had woken her.

But just as she lay back, a different sound breached the gaps between the howling wind and the slap of the waves. It was familiar yet strange and it was hard to focus on, through the noise of the storm.

She sat up again and crept to the window. She felt an unease growing in the pit of her stomach but wasn't sure why. So instead of looking out the window, she knelt below it, her ear held close to the edge of the stone window sill.

The sound was intermittent, a low hum punctuated by silence and the effects of the weather. But she thought it was getting louder. Coming closer.

After a few moments, either *it* grew louder or *she* was able to focus in on it enough to distinguish what it was. Voices. *Male* voices.

They're back!, she thought. *But so soon?*

She began dressing as fast as she could; jeans and an old hoodie, on top of the t-shirt and shorts she was already wearing. As she fumbled around in the dark for her flashlight, she realised the voices seemed to have quietened.

Probably don't want to wake us, she thought.

She hurried down the stairs and pulled on her shoes, bouncing up and down as she lost balance. Finally ready and curious as to why the journey up to the big house was taking so long, she flung open the front door and then staggered back in shock and horror.

Just outside the door were three men, their faces almost as shocked as hers, eyes winced at the bright light from her flashlight. The mutual shock of both parties lasted only an instant, but it was just long enough for Maisie, acting on sheer reaction rather than conscious thought, to fling the front door shut.

There were no locks on that or any other door on the island, but it gave her the extra moment she needed for her mind to catch up with her body. She *knew* these men. Or she thought she did anyway. These were no lost strangers. They were terrors in the night.

The door handle turned and Maisie bolted through the house, into the kitchen and out through the back into the pouring rain. She paused at the rear door just long enough to hear heavy footsteps behind her, pounding fast in her wake. *No time to wake the others,* she thought. *Maybe I can draw them away.*

Without much of a plan she tore up and out of the rear garden and hard up the slope towards the top of the island. *Not around the side of the house, one of them could be coming that way.*

'WAIT!' she heard a voice shout behind her. It was a voice filled with gravel and anger.

She knew the men were pursuing, could feel it in her bones and almost hear their grunts. But she also knew the island like the back of her hand, a clear advantage in the thick dark of the moonless atlantic predawn. She clicked her flashlight off, prayed not to trip on any rocks and raced hard past the reservoir and across the slope of the island, from one coast to the other.

Before she did anything else, she wanted to see the vessel the men had arrived in and whether there were any more of them. She knew there was no way down from the east cliff of the island to the beach, but her flashlight was a powerful one, top of the range, and she thought it would illuminate the shore enough to see from a high position.

As she ran hard across the shoddy ground, her heart beating a mallet against her chest and her throat burning from the cold air, she could sense the men falling behind. One of them had given a yelp as his foot got caught in a divot and he went down. She had almost gone down herself once or twice. Almost.

She didn't know if they were still pursuing her or not and she knew it didn't matter anyway: there was no way off the island. But for all the instinctiveness in her decision to run, this part was at least working.

When she reached the far end of the island, she followed the cliff line down and around, until she was facing the shore. She lay down on her front and tried to calm her breathing enough to listen for any sound of the intruders. *Nothing.*

She felt the fabric of her clothing damp against her and noticed the rain for the first time. The ground she lay on was soaking too. It was a wonder she hadn't slipped over. A wonder and a mercy.

She brought the flashlight around in front of her face and paused. *Once I turn this on, they'll know where I am,* she thought. *What next?*

As she lay there though, her mind racing, she noticed dim pinpoints of light down by the shore. Two of them were white and the other was red. *Boat lights,* she thought. They weren't bright enough to illuminate the boat, their intention was merely to let other vessels know of its presence and avoid a deadly nighttime collision. But they gave her an idea of the boat's size. It was bigger than Steve's, but not too much bigger. *Enough to carry a few men and supplies, but not an army,* she thought.

She scanned the horizon, looking for signs of any other boats either near the shore or further out.

There were none.

Ok, she thought. *At least three of them, but not too many more. Not the whole gang. If it is them. Oh god, what if it is?*

Her mind flashed with grim memories and fear. She had to be sure.

She aimed her flashlight at the rear of the boat, where the red light was glowing in a wall of black. *Just one second,* she thought. *On and off and then get the hell out of here.*

She flicked the flashlight on. And then, heart sinking into the muddy earth beneath her, she flicked it off again. It was them.

18

The flag flying from the rear of the boat was unmistakable. A black sheet with a white skull in the middle and two crossed cutlasses underneath. In many ways it was a ridiculous thing; a cheap novelty found in gift shops all over the world. But what had once been feared, only to be worn or carried in jest years later, was now something to be feared again.

Is there a tipping point in years where a symbol of violence and hatred can become a thing of mirth and merriment? Is one symbol worse than another? Or are they just symbols? Perhaps old symbols of fear and death should be banned and left to die, lest they be used again one day for immoral motives. Or perhaps the biggest injury to those who fly under such banners, is for those banners to be used again for jokes and parties years later. Who is to say?

Although Maisie had only had her light on for the briefest of moments, she knew that any bright light on the island at night would be like a beacon in the dark for those who were looking. She heard an indistinguishable shout below, a clatter of boots on creaking wood and then a large beam of light cut through the dark, illuminating the slope right beside her. *The fog lamp,* she thought. *I guess they left it off to catch us by surprise. No need for them to hide anymore.*

The shaft of dazzling light swept over her head and off the far Eastern edge of the island. She pressed herself hard into the ground. *Why didn't I get moving when I had the chance?*

The light swept past her again, closer this time. But before making its return pass, a voice called out from beyond the shore. A woman's voice.

The light flung around to illuminate a female form, shielding her eyes with both arms from the devastating glare.

No! thought Maisie. *Oh god Karen, no.*

19

As grim as it had felt waking up that first morning on the island, waking up on the first morning back on the mainland was far worse.

I had lain awake most of the night, mind racing and struck deep by anxiety and the creeping desperation of our plight. In spite of my perilous journey to St. Rita, the non-stop adrenaline of the first few days, the terrible news on the radio and the comfort of finding new allies in the struggle for survival, I had always held on to the hope of returning to normality on the mainland one day. It was a hope shrouded in denial and I had kept it buried deep in the lowest reaches of my subconscious. But that dream had been smashed by Jimmy's story. The painful truth splintering any hope I had left into a billion tiny pieces.

I had finally fallen into a fitful sleep just a couple of hours from daybreak. Once the grey light of dawn appeared, I was ripped from the comfort of slumber and back into the world. The hopelessness washed over me immediately, even more painful than the banging in my head and the soreness in my eyes.

This would be my last trip to the mainland. And it would need to be a quick one, if we were to avoid being irradiated to the point of no return. If I survived many more years, they would be lived out on the island, clinging to that icy rock in the north atlantic, scratching desperately to stay alive.

But the island was something. It was a life. And there was Maisie. If it hadn't been for her in that moment, I may well have chosen Jimmy's path - hunkering down to await the inevitable.

Instead I pushed myself into an upright position, sat on the edge of the bed for a moment, held my head in my hands to fight off the nausea, and then stood up, composed myself and made my way out of the room. Jake was nowhere to be found upstairs, but small sounds from below suggested he was already up and about.

I headed downstairs and stopped at the edge of the living room, not sure if I should interrupt the scene in front of me.

Jimmy was laid flat out on the sofa, Jake beside him in a chair he'd dragged over, a bowl of something that looked like beans in one hand and a spoon in the other. He was trying to encourage Jimmy to eat. I wondered if he'd asked about Duncan yet.

Jake glanced up at me and nodded. *It's hopeless. But join us anyway won't you?*

I took my seat from the night before and sat in silence as Jimmy made a valiant effort to stifle his coughing and retching just long enough to take a few mouthfuls. Eventually and not without considerable effort, he sat up. Jake remained by his side, the deep dark bags under his eyes suggesting he'd had about as much luck sleeping as I'd had.

Jimmy nodded his thanks. Then with a small smile to me and a croaky voice said 'Morning's are the worst. I'm usually ok once I get the day underway.'

I admired his courage but read between the lines: *each morning gets worse.*

'I need to ask you something Jimmy,' Jake said, in a gentle but firm voice. 'It's the reason we're here.'

Jimmy returned his attention to Jake. 'Of course,' he said.

'Have you seen or heard anything from Duncan? Duncan McRae?' he fought hard to keep the urgency from his voice and I was relieved to see that he had well understood the gravity of the situation.

'Duncan,' Jimmy repeated. He thought for a moment before continuing, his voice growing stronger with every sentence.

'The last I'd heard of him was that the Pirates had got a hold of him. For the most part the gang either forced people to work for them or intimidated them into giving up supplies. But nobody saw or heard from Duncan again after that, so I don't know whether they killed him or he escaped. Either way, I'm sorry Jake, I just don't know.'

Jake stared hard at the ground. I remained silent, conscious of the tipping point he had now reached. Either we gave up now and turned back, or we risked our own lives and a slow, painful death for a man who may not even himself, be alive.

'There is someone who might know though. If he's still alive that is,' Jimmy offered.

Jake's head shot up and he stared at Jimmy, imploring him to go on.

'Young Mike Finbough was forced to tend field for the Pirates for some time before they fled. If they took Duncan, he might have seen or heard something from them.'

'Where would Mike be now?' Jake asked, his face a picture of strain and desperation.

'He never left the farm they had him working on. He continued tending it until the animals began dying and he himself got sick. Helped a lot of people who were left behind in the village.'

'Which Farm? How far from here?'

'Mason's. A ways out, on the other side of the town.'

Jake's face fell. 'I know it,' he said, returning his gaze to the floor.

I realised that even though he knew where it was, Jake had calculated that it would take us too long to walk there and back. It was too risky a thing to do on a mere hope.

'We could take my car?' Jimmy said. I stared at him in shock. He had simultaneously ruined and then saved our day in a heartbeat.

'You have a car?' I asked, unable to keep the incredulity out of my voice.

'Aye,' he said. 'I hid it around the back when I

moved down here. It's got just enough gas in it for one last journey. Only a short one, mind. I don't know what I was saving it for, but it felt like a good idea in case those Pirates ever returned.'

'Will it still go?' Jake asked.

Jimmy nodded. 'I've kept it running,' he said. 'Turned it over every week or so, just to make sure. Keys are behind the books on the shelf in the kitchen.'

Jake shot up and then caught himself. 'Are you sure Jimmy?'

'Look at me Jake,' he said, shaking his head. 'I've got no use for it. I'd ask you to take me with you though. Wherever you're going, I'd like to die making a go of it, rather than stuck here in my pit.'

It was the least we could do. Jake went to fetch the keys.

20

Karen had realised her mistake the moment she saw them. In the half a minute or so it had taken her eyes to adjust to the stinging light from the fog lamp, they had sprinted up the hill and grabbed a hold of her. She smelt their rancid breath and saw the cruelty in their eyes as she struggled against their grip.

'Karen isn't it? It's so good to see you again,' the leader said, a grin on his unshaven face.

She recognised the voice immediately. It was the man from the radio. Tim, the ringleader of the Pirates. She'd had a nagging thought that the voice had been familiar but it had been hard to tell over the spit and crackle of the radio. Now that he was in front of her though, it all fell crashing into place.

But despite her horror, she still held out a small hope that they might have brought her brother with them. It was a hope that was dashed harder than the storm surge crashing against the rocks, the moment she asked them though. And all she was left with was fear and hopelessness.

21

Once she'd seen the gang grab Karen and drag her back to the big house, Maisie was faced with a tough decision.

There was nowhere to hide on the island. She could probably avoid them until daybreak, but as soon as it got light they would easily be able to find her. There was no way off the island either, short of somehow stealing the Pirate's boat. And even if she thought she could pull that off, she would never leave Karen and the others behind. Especially her niece and nephew.

She couldn't hope to fight them off alone. Together, they might be able to overpower the gang but they would need a plan and the element of surprise. And that would take time. Her priority had to be the others and that meant she would need to go back to the big house, surrender and hope for the best.

But she'd heard the stories and had seen what these ruthless men could do. Throwing her fate into their hands was not an easy thing to accept.

The sun had begun to rise when she made her decision. Cold, wet and shaking with adrenaline, she trudged back across the island.

22

After a short drive through the empty streets of the village and out the other end back into the countryside, Jake pulled Jimmy's car up outside a large farmhouse. There was a huge barn to the right and several smaller outhouses dotted around the muddy driveway.

A sign above the front door in flaking green paint said "Mason's Farm", but most of the letters were obscured by a tattered Jolly Roger, which had been hung above it crudely with old bits of electrical wire.

'Are you sure they're gone?' I asked Jimmy. I didn't like the look of the place one bit.

'Aye,' Jimmy said. 'As soon as they packed up and left, the news went around. It was a big relief for the rest of us. Despite all the sickness abound.'

I nodded, but still felt uneasy as I stared at the farmhouse. The place had a feeling about it. A misery growing up through the ground along with the weeds.

On the drive over, Jimmy had asked again where we'd come from. Jake couldn't misdirect any longer and I got the sense he didn't want to. And neither did I for that matter. If you couldn't trust a man like Jimmy, a man at death's door who still tried to help you despite having lost everything, who could you trust?

Jake had given him the brief version; Duncan telling them about the island, being forced to leave him behind, meeting me on that first morning, settling into some form of a life. He left out the part where I threatened them with a gun and tried to force them away.

Jimmy hadn't said much in response. He just stared out the window, coughing slightly as the damp grey landscape passed by. Shortly before we pulled up the farm track he said, 'I'm happy for you Jake. Happy at least some of us will survive this.' I could tell he meant it and was grateful to him again, for his constant graciousness.

We sat in the car for a minute, looking for anything that might indicate the place hadn't been abandoned. There was no doubt anyone in the house would have heard us coming - the storm had died down and the engine of the car was the only noise for miles. But no one appeared at a door or window, or came around the side of the barn. Still we were cautious though.

'You better come with us if you can Jimmy,' Jake said. 'Better anyone here sees you first, in case they get the wrong idea.'

Jimmy nodded and struggled to push himself

upright in the seat.

I opened the door and stepped out, one hand reaching behind me to grasp the butt of the rifle, watching the house. Jake helped Jimmy out and looked another unspoken message to me: *I'll watch Jimmy, you watch us.* I understood and nodded my acknowledgement. Together they made their way toward the farmhouse and I followed, a few paces behind them. Every sense in my body was on high alert and my skin tingled in the breeze.

When we got to the door, Jimmy said 'Try the door Jakey-boy, I'll head through first. I'll be ok on my cane.'

Jake let Jimmy go and turned the handle on the front door. It opened first time. No need for security when everyone was dead or dying I supposed.

Jimmy staggered through with Jake hot on his heels. He raised a hand behind his back indicating for me to hold by the door. Jimmy and Jake might be a bearable surprise for any occupants inside who might recognise them, but a stranger with a gun was another thing entirely.

After a few moments Jake's voice carried to me from deep inside the house.

'Hello? Anybody in here?' and then after a couple more beats: 'Carl.'

I stepped inside and followed the sound to a big room at the back of the house. The stench was awful, a mixture of mold, rotting food and death. The hallway was covered in a dark, patterned wallpaper, torn in several places, and the carpet was threadbare and stained with god knows what. The very walls seemed to scream in horror at what they had seen.

Inside the room looked like a burglary had taken place. Most of the furniture was upended, there were deep scars in the walls and broken glass on the floor. Jimmy was perched on a scant wooden chair by the wall, while Jake knelt over what looked like a pile of cushions, blankets and dirty clothing in the far corner of the room. He was staring intently at the messy pile, concern on his face.

I stood and watched for a moment, my ears remaining alert to any sound.

'Dead is he?' Jimmy said. There was no surprise in his voice. I realised there was the shape of a body underneath the pile.

Jake reached out to check for a pulse. There was a groan and the pile moved. Jake shot back and both Jimmy and I jumped.

'Christ, he's alive,' Jake said, before regaining his composure and kneeling back down.

I walked over to Jake's side and stood there, frozen to the spot at the sight before me.

Jake had pulled back the covers and what lay beneath looked like a corpse. Except its eyes were fixed on Jake's and its lips were moving up and down silently.

'Mike?,' Jake said, 'Can you hear me?'

Mike was alive but barely. His face didn't look like a face at all, just a blotchy mess of red and white. It was as though his flesh and skin was melting from his skull. My stomach turned at the sight. The poor man.

Jake asked again and Mike managed to nod his head slightly, once up and once down.

'Is there anybody else here Mike?' Jake asked. 'Anyone upstairs or outside?'

'Nughh' Mike managed. *No.*

Jimmy stared at the floor, unable to look at what his own fate had instore for him.

Jake looked up at me, as if unsure what to do next. I crouched down beside him and turned my face so that I was just behind his back and could whisper to him.

'We haven't got long Jake. This is our best chance. Probably our last chance.' I tried not to sound unsympathetic. I was anything but. But we *couldn't* stay much longer. With or without Duncan, we had to get back to the island, or face being irradiated ourselves.

From the corner of my eye I saw Jake nod his head.

'Michael, I need to ask you something. My brother-in-law Duncan… Duncan McRae. Have you seen him? Do you know where he might be?'

Mike's eyes were watching Jake like a baby staring at a brightly coloured mobile. He seemed to recognise Jake, but there was no way to be sure. He began moving again, writhing around in small movements, face filled with the strain of trying to talk.

'Gu-ahh…' It was more of an exhale than an actual word.

'It's ok, take your time.' Jake placed a hand on

his chest. My heart was breaking and racing at the same time. Mike continued his silent struggle.

'G-ua… gone. De-ead.' he said. Jake's head dropped.

Mike's body twitched and shook as a wracking cough overcame him from the effort of trying to speak. It lasted several moments and then with a groan, Michael himself, was gone.

'I'm sorry Michael. I'm so sorry.' Jake's voice broke almost imperceptibly and he swallowed hard to keep his composure.

23

Tim Fairbrother's voice rang in Karen's head through the rest of the night, into dawn and clear into the morning.

She kept replaying the scene over and over in her head.

The leader of the Pirates had smiled deeply when she'd asked if her brother was with them.

'Duncan? Oh no Karen, he's long gone.'

She'd had to know. And so she'd asked what had happened to him. But she would wish she hadn't. She would hear his reply and the sickening laugh of his men over and over again in her mind for the rest of her life.

'Wouldn't tell us where you'd gone, see. And old Greig here is an amateur torturer at best. Went too far. *Way* too far.'

Tim and his men dragged her back to the big house and rounded up the others, who'd been woken by the commotion and staggered outside into sheer hell. The children began screaming when they saw the men and caught sight of Tim's crude shotgun and the large knives his men brandished.

Tim ordered Karen to shut them up. Steve made to reason with them, hands held palm upwards in front of him. 'We're no danger to you. Please… take anything you want, just don't hurt my family.' he said.

Tim pushed the gun under Steve's chin and forced him back against the wall of the big house.

'Listen here pal,' his voice was not raised, but was filled with malice. 'We're not going anywhere and we don't need your permission, understood?' Steve was held stiff, his hands pressed against the wall and his feet on tip-toes as the gun pressed hard into the underside of his chin. He was too shocked to respond.

'Is that understood?' the leader repeated, this time louder and with a jerk of the shotgun to emphasise the question. Steve strained hard to give a minimal nod of his head up and down. *Yes.*

'Good. Me and my lads here are not unreasonable people,' he said with a smile. 'And we're not in the business of hurting children. But that can change, I assure you.'

'Ok!' Susan said, clutching Tom and Aileen between her and Karen. 'We'll do whatever you say. Please just lower the gun.' she begged.

Tim lowered the gun slowly, keeping his eyes fixed hard on Steve, who sank down to sit on his ankles against the wall.

'I don't know what you've been up to out here, but there's going to be some changes on this island.

From now on you only speak when spoken to. What we say goes. No questions, no quibbles. Got it?'

Nobody answered, but Susan nodded her head and raised her hand slightly from Tom's chest to signal that they all understood.

After that they had been herded into the living room and made to sit on the floor. Tim told his boys to search upstairs for anyone else and when they returned alone, he turned to Karen.

'Is this all of you? Where's that lanky husband of yours? Hiding out with Maisie somewhere?'

Susan thought quickly and answered for her: 'He went looking for another island yesterday. Took the boat with him. Somewhere with some trees or wood or something. We need to make some repairs and there's no trees anywhere on the island.' she realised she was rambling and hoped they didn't see through her half-truth.

He looked at her for a moment, before deciding it was a reasonable enough story to be true.

'We'll have to be vigilant for his triumphant return then. Well, let's hope it's triumphant anyway. This place could do with a fix up.'

He told Greig to watch them and went back outside with the other gang member.

Karen wasn't sure how long they'd sat there like that, Susan stroking the hair of the little ones and trying to soften their whimpering. After some time, there was a commotion outside. Then the door flew open and Maisie was flung onto the ground beside them. She was soaked from head to toe and looked like she'd been dragged through a bush. She sat up slowly, regained her composure and scooted closer to the group, fixing her eyes on the floor.

'Now we're all back together, I'll tell you what I told them,' Tim said, focusing on Maisie. 'There'll be no more fucking around. You go where we tell you and you do what we tell you to do. I'm not a patient guy and there will be no second chances. If you do what we say then we all might get along and live a long and happy life together. Got it?'

He placed a hand under Masie's chin and gripped her jaw, yanking her gaze up to him.

'That goes double for you princess. My boys here have been without company for some time. They'll be restrained as long as I tell 'em to be. But any more mischief and you're on your own.'

Maisie nodded and he pushed her head back so hard that she fell backwards. He was testing her and she knew it. He wanted her to resist so he could take pleasure in punishing her. So she simply sat back up again and resumed her vigil of the dusty floor.

'You!,' Tim said, pointing at Steve. 'Come with us, we've got a job for you.'

Steve rose on unsteady legs.

'Where are you taking him?' Susan asked, unable to keep her voice from rising. Tim smacked her hard across the face and she fell back across the floor. The kids screamed.

'Final warning,' he said. 'Now, if I remember correctly, Karen, you're a nurse?'

Karen nodded. 'Yes,' she said. It was all she

could manage.

'Good,' he said. He made his way to the door and motioned to Steve to follow. Steve hesitated, looking at Susan, who lay on the floor holding the side of her face.

'Well, come on!' he said, looking back at him from the door frame.

Steve broke his gaze, helped Susan up and then walked past Tim and out the door, his heads held down to avoid his glare.

'The rest of you stay here. We've got some work to do but it won't take long. When I get back I'll find you all sitting here just like this, or one of you is going for a long swim. I'm sure I don't need to remind you that there's nowhere to run.' And with that he followed the others out and slammed the door behind him. It groaned hard on its rusty hinges and threatened to fall off.

After a few minutes, when she was sure they were gone, Susan began to sob.

'I'm so sorry,' she said, through tears and gasps for air.

24

Maisie's expression darkened as Karen explained it all to her and the others. But she didn't say anything in response. Her mind was still racing through their situation, running through options and testing them out in her head. So far she hadn't come up with anything failproof.

'How could you?' Susan asked when Karen finished. Her eyes were wet too, but the tears were held back by her shock at Karen's story and her urge not to worry the children any more than they already were.

Karen said nothing in reply, just shook her head from left to right as her body wracked with uncontrollable sobbing. Her children wrapped their arms around her, not entirely sure what was happening, but wanting to comfort their mother.

'It's ok,' Maisie finally said, through gritted teeth that she hoped weren't showing. 'We just need to bide our time and make a plan. There's more of us then them and Jake and Carl will be back soon.' The thought brought an urgent question to her mind: 'Have they asked about Jake yet? Do they know about Carl?'

Susan shook her head. 'No, they don't. When they gathered us up they asked if this was all of us and I told them Jake had gone looking for wood by himself.'

'Good thinking,' Maise said. She looked at Karen. 'Are you sure you didn't say anything about Carl?'

Karen didn't meet her gaze. 'No I don't think so. I don't think I mentioned him.'

'Ok,' Maisie said. 'We'll need to think of a way to distract them when Jake and Carl get back. They'll hear the boat coming and think they have the element of surprise. That will be the moment to act. Getting one of the guns will be our priority. Don't hesitate to shoot if you get one. We need to be ready.'

Susan didn't have a chance to respond as they heard the front door swing open. They could hear grunts and coughing, but no one came into the living room. Instead they heard the stairs groan as if something heavy was being carried up them.

After some bangs and bumps from above them, they heard steps coming back down the stairs and held their breath.

Greig came into the living room, shut the door behind him and simply stood there watching them.

The memory of the sting from the leader's slap was still fresh in her mind, but Susan was worried about her husband and couldn't hold back. 'Is everything ok?' she asked.

'Quiet' he said. They obeyed.

A few moments later there was a knock on the door and Greig opened it to let Steve back into the room.

Maisie looked at Steve as he sat down close to Susan and took hold of her hand. Their heads pressed together and they stared at the floor in front of them. Maisie wanted to make eye contact with him in a vain attempt to understand what was going on. But he didn't notice her, so she looked him over instead. He didn't look like he'd come to any more harm. Neither did he seem alarmed by whatever the gang had had him do. Well, at least not any more alarmed than they already were anyway.

After some time there was the sound of heavy boots coming down creaking wooden stairs again and Tim entered the room. He pointed at Karen and barked 'You, come with me.' and turned his finger around into a hook to emphasise the point.

'What do you want with her?' Maisie asked, more forcefulness in her voice than she had intended. He glanced at her, an angry growl on his unshaven face. And… was that a tear in his eye?

'Greig,' he commanded, turning away and heading out the door.

Greig stalked over and kicked Maisie hard in the side. 'I said quiet!' he yelled. He grabbed Karen under the shoulder and she yelped as he pulled her to her feet.

Steve raised his hands, palms outward in a gesture of supplication. He had learned the hard way about speaking out of turn but still felt the need to do something to cool the anger of the gang and calm the rest of the group.

Greig gave him a look and Steve gently outstretched his fingers and nodded as if to say *we're ok here, just take it easy... please.*

It seemed to do the trick and Greig released his grip on Karen's arm.

'Am I going to get any more trouble from you?' he grunted to her. She shook her head, eyes fixed firmly on the ground.

'Good.' He gestured towards the door and she walked out to join Tim, her footsteps small and uncertain. Maisie watched them until the door was shut once again and Greig resumed his place in front of it. She heard the sound of steps heading upwards again. Tim's heavy boots followed by Karen's lighter steps.

Four of them, she thought. *But one of them's sick. And that's important to Tim somehow. That's why he needs Karen.*

25

Though I knew nothing of Mike and his life before then, his death, there in front of us on the floor of a filthy house at the edge of a dying world, was heartbreaking. Were it not for the pounding urgency, which had begun the morning as a low murmur and grown to a deafening drum beat in my chest, I would have wanted to give him a proper burial. From the looks of Jake, he felt the same.

'Jake,' I said. It was a one word sentence, which I tried not to sound like an order. I didn't need to say the rest. *We have to get out of here.*

Jake wiped his eyes with the back of his palm and nodded. He crossed Mike's arms over his chest and made to stand.

'This is my fate isn't it?' Jimmy asked, to neither of us in particular. It wasn't really a question. His eyes had glazed over and he was staring at the wall.

'We don't know that Jimmy,' Jake said. 'It could be Mike has an infection or…' the lie died in his throat. Mike's death had brought the loss of his own previous life hard into vision. He had about as much motivation left in his tank as I did.

'Jimmy,' I said, 'You've been good to us and I mean you no ill. But if we don't get away from here soon, it will be our fate too. I'm sorry.'

Jake glared hard at me but Jimmy nodded his head.

'I understand. I don't want to slow you down. If you have someplace you can go to avoid this…' he gestured around the room. He didn't mean Mike's death specifically, but more everything - what the world had become. 'Then you *must* go there. But please, bring me with you for as long as you can. I don't want to die alone.'

There was no hesitation from either of us. We would carry Jimmy back to the car, onto the boat and, if he made it that far, back to the island. It was too late to save him, but we owed him that much.

But we had to move fast now. Jimmy made to stand but Jake and I grabbed him, wrapping an arm each around our shoulders. We carried him back out to the car and got him settled in the back seat. Then we flung ourselves in the front, Jake at the wheel. He tore the old machine into reverse, turned and then accelerated hard back towards the road. I prayed we had enough fuel to get back to the boat. I wasn't exactly sure how much exposure we'd had at the point, but I felt sure that if we had to walk back to shore it would be too late.

26

Karen's mind eased when she entered the room. She'd followed Tim upstairs fearing the worst, but hoping he wanted her medical expertise rather than… something else. He had asked her if she was a nurse after all, and she thought maybe he had an injury he wanted her help with. Although she saw no visible sign of one on him. But when she followed him into the room and he stood aside and gestured to the cot bed, she understood. And was relieved.

A man lay there, wrapped in the dirtiest of blankets and not moving, save for the unsteady rise and fall of his chest.

'My brother's sick,' Tim said. 'Do what you need to do to fix him. We have a load of medicines. Whatever you need.' He motioned to an old sea chest in the corner and a duffle bag on top of it. The zip was broken and a couple of small white boxes had fallen out.

She walked over to the man in the cot, aware

of the intensity of Tim's gaze as she did. She knelt beside him and in spite of her fear and wrought nerves, her many years of training and experience kicked in.

'What's his name?' she asked, as she placed the back of her hand against the man's forehead. He was burning up.

'Alan.' Tim said.

'Alan?' she asked, her voice quiet and compassionate but firm. 'Alan, my name's Karen. Can you hear me?'

Alan didn't respond. He was still alive, but she could tell just from looking at him that he was in very bad shape indeed. The kind of shape that no amount of medicine would fix. But she had to do something to show she was trying. She had a feeling her safety and that of the others relied upon it.

So she pulled down the blanket and reached for his wrist, taking his pulse. She counted off the numbers in her head.

'Taking his pulse won't help. What does he *need*?' Tim growled, growing impatient. But Karen was used to impatient, worried family members and she simply raised her hand to quiet him while she kept track of Alan's pulse. She was a nurse again, confident in her abilities and assuring in her care. It was a relief to assume her former role and all her fear and guilt melted away into the background.

Content with what she felt, she let his arm rest back by his side and then rested her ear gently against his chest. Tim was still staring at her with restless eyes.

'I need a pen and something to write on,' she said. He stared back at her, incredulous. So she went on, never raising her head from his chest. 'I need to keep track of his vital signs while I treat him. It's the only way to check his improvement and I can't do it all by memory.' She used her best nurse's voice. And it worked.

'Wait here,' he said and left the room to find what she needed.

No longer under his intent glare, she became aware of the awful smell of the man in front of her. It was clear he hadn't washed for weeks, possibly even months and had probably been in the same clothes for that period too. She held her breath and focused on his breathing. It was uneven and rasping.

She withdrew her head and then placed her thumb on his eyelid, lifting it slowly. He recoiled slightly and then was still again. *Ok*, she thought, *he's not quite at death's door, but it won't be too long before he is.*

She glanced at the room around her. A blanket had been draped over the window and a large, upended torch stood in the corner, providing light for the room. She needed a torch, but that one was much too big for her purposes. She crawled over to the duffle bag and rifled around the bag through boxes, medicine tubs, bandages and other medical paraphernalia. No joy. She checked the outer pockets and found what she was looking for - a small maglite.

Returning to his side, she again placed her thumb on the man's eyelid. Slower this time, she lifted it and pointed the small torch at his bloodshot eye. His pupil contracted against the light and he pulled away again, but made no sound. She looked at his face in the dim light from the torch. It was blotchy, red and white in patches and raised in several places.

She hadn't seen radiation sickness before but she was sure that was what it was. Unless he had an injury somewhere that was infected, but then she thought Tim would have pointed that out already. She decided to check him anyway, just to be sure. She pulled down the blankets and searched his clothes for any signs of blood. Finding none, she pulled up his thick woolen jumper and the t-shirt underneath. The skin on his stomach was the same as that on his face, but even worse.

'What are you doing?' Tim had returned and stood clutching a biro and what looked like a piece of card torn from the side of a box. His voice made her jump, but she regained her composure quickly.

'Examining him,' she said in a cool, firm voice that she hoped brooked no more questions. 'Has he got any injuries that I should be aware of?'

'Injuries? No. He's obviously sick, what kind of a nurse are you?'

'It's a standard question,' she said. 'The smallest infection on an unseen wound can look just like an illness.'

This seemed to take him back and perhaps give him confidence that his brother was being treated by someone who knew what they were doing.

'No. No, I don't think so,' he said. 'He's been coughing a lot and there's been a bit of blood, but he's been conscious up until recently and he hasn't complained of any injury.'

'We should check,' Karen said. 'And get him out of these clothes. Will you help me?'

Tim nodded. He placed the pen and piece of card at the foot of the bed and then helped Karen disrobe Alan. Karen used the mini-torch to look all over his body. There were no visible injuries, not even a scratch, but there were the same blotches all over his skin.

Karen thought for a moment. 'Do you have any Iodine?'

She knew it was far too late to save him, but she had to give the impression that she thought she could.

'I think so,' Tim said. He went over to the bag and tipped its contents onto the floor, flipping one box or bottle over at a time, reading the labels. Finding what he was looking for he handed the box to Karen and stood staring at his brother. He spoke in a measured tone without lifting his gaze from Alan. 'Just so you know Karen. If he doesn't make a full recovery, your little group here will suffer the consequences.'

Karen nodded. 'No pressure darling!' he clapped her on the back with a forced grin.

27

The roads were empty apart from the wet leaves which flew up behind us as we sped along. It felt as if the whole world were empty and we were the sole survivors, pursued by a beast that was all around us, but which we could not see.

The rain had begun to fall again by the time we made it back to the boat. It was only a light drizzle, but the breeze that carried with it was enough to stir the sea up into an angry broth. It lashed the boat in uneven fashion and made it hard for us to get Jimmy aboard safely. Everything felt like it was taking too long.

We were coming back empty handed, but that thought barely crossed our minds. Nothing we could lay our hands on would be safe to bring back anyway and the overriding sensation was that we had to get away. For the second time I was making a mad dash for the island of St. Rita. But this would be the last time I would be back on the mainland, and I knew it.

Soaked to the knees with seawater and above them with rain, Jake and I did our best to make Jimmy comfortable on the deck and then we cast off, Jake firing the engines for all they were worth.

We rode the waves, smashing over and through the coastal waters and out into the open ocean. I clung to the side of the boat, the memory of going overboard that first night brought crashing back to the forefront of my mind. This was a far sturdier boat of course and Jake an excellent captain, but in spite of this and in spite of the fact that the mainland was drifting away behind us, I still had a deep feeling of dread. I should have been feeling relieved, but I wasn't. I told myself over and over again that we'd be ok, that we'd made it off the mainland in time. But I couldn't shake the feeling that something was wrong. It stayed with me through the day and into the night as we journeyed back.

Perhaps it was a premonition and perhaps not. I'm not sure I believe in such things. But when Jake suddenly killed the engine and shut the lights off, calling out to me in an urgent whisper through the darkness, I realised I was right to be concerned. Something was very wrong.

28

As we left the mainland, back on the island Karen had been ordered to remain by the sick man's side at all times. After some consideration though, Tim had decided to let Maisie and the others go about their business. He reasoned that they weren't about to go anywhere and his gang were low on food, so if the group had their little farm to work, they may as well get on with it. There would be more mouths to feed now. At least for a short while anyway.

Maisie kept quiet, but took note of everything. Tim had posted Greig down by the dock while he and the other man, Paul, boarded their vessel to rest. So she figured the Pirates would take it in shifts to guard her and the others. Staying on the boat instead of the house had been smart - if the group decided to rush Greig and somehow manage to subdue him, the others would be roused in plenty of time to fight back. And they were the only ones on the island with a gun.

We need a plan, she thought, time and again in her head. She reminded herself to be patient and not try to force anything, but she was acutely aware that time was limited. Their best opportunity would come when the others returned and she knew it. But she had no idea when that would be.

She also knew she would have to be careful in how she communicated the plan to the rest of the group. Although they'd now been given a fair amount of freedom, if any of them were caught in deep conversation rather than going about their chores, it would arouse suspicion. So when the others came to her by the small farm they had built inside the dome, she forced them away. 'We'll talk while we work,' she'd said. 'Never in a huddle like this. Plus I need some time to think.'

The others had deferred to her for leadership in the absence of Jake. She didn't know why, but she was determined no to let them down. And so they worked through the day while she thought. They tended the crops and then took turns working on the channel, or carrying water down the hill. They rested in turns too. It had been a long night for all of them and they were tired.

The reservoir was as far as they were permitted to go. Originally Tim had told them to stay between the house and the farm. Everywhere else was a no-go and they would be shot on sight if they were seen outside of those areas. But Maisie had calmly convinced them that the reservoir was a must too and they had acquiesced.

The restrictions meant that any attempt to walk down to the dock would be seen as a breach of the rules. She had considered arguing this point as well, on account of them needing to catch fish once in a while, but had decided against it. *One small victory at a time. Don't push it.*

The route down to the dock from the big house was covered some of the way by the outhouse opposite. But there was still some 200 metres down past the row of houses on the left where anyone attempting to get to the shore would be in full view of the dock. There was a small, dilapidated stone wall on the right side of the wide path, which might cover a crouching person some more of the way. But the last 50 metres or so had fallen away almost completely onto the rocks below and there was no shelter there. So any frontal assault would still be in full view of the dock and the boat for long enough to get off a couple of shots.

In the late afternoon Maisie risked going to speak to Karen. She found her in the bedroom upstairs, laid out on a blanket and dosing beside a cot bed with what looked like a very sick man in it. She paused at the door, not sure if the man was a danger or not. He wasn't moving, save for the uneven rise and fall of his chest.

'Karen,' she whispered.

Karen raised her head but had to wipe the bleariness from her eyes before she could make out the shape of Maisie at the door.

'Maisie? What's going on?' she sounded alarmed.

Maisie came toward her one palm raised to indicate that there was no need for panic. She sat on the floor opposite Karen and nodded a question toward the man in the cot bed.

'He's Tim's brother. It's ok, he's very sick. Barely conscious.'

Maisie nodded. 'What's wrong with him?' she asked

'I can't be a hundred percent, but I think it's radiation sickness. He's a long way gone Maisie. Two to three days at most I'd say. And if he dies…' her voice trailed off.

Maisie looked at him. Karen didn't have to say any more. It made more sense now - the rest of them had come to little harm so far, but only because Tim needed Karen to treat his brother. As long as his brother was alive they would be relatively safe.

'Does he know? That it's a lost cause I mean?'

'No. I've steered clear of the subject and focused on an elaborate treatment plan. But it's all nonsense Maisie. I'm not a doctor and we don't even have a tenth of what we need to even make him comfortable. I don't know what I'm going to do.' Tears welled up in her eyes.

Maisie placed a hand on her shoulder. 'You're doing great Karen. Just keep him alive for as long as you can. I'll figure something out.'

'The guys will be back soon. What will he do to Jake if I can't keep him alive?' she was sobbing now and in danger of hyperventilating.

'Karen, look at me. You have to control what you can control. They don't know about Carl yet and that gives us something. But we don't know when they'll be back and you need to give us as much time as you can ok? Just focus on that and let me take care of the rest.'

Karen calmed and wiped her eyes on the sleeve of her dirty pink jumper.

'Ok,' she said, in a small voice.

'I've got to get back to the group. Are you going to be alright?'

Karen nodded. 'Yes. Go. I'll be ok.'

Maisie gave her a quick hug and left the room. Her mind began racing again. *Two to three days. Max. I've got to think fast.*

And that's what she did. By the end of the day she had a rough plan. It was a good one and probably would have worked too, if we hadn't gotten back earlier than she expected.

29

‘Carl!’

Jake’s voice strained as he tried to whisper and shout the name at the same time. My eyes had yet to adjust to the sudden darkness and I had to feel my way along the side of the boat and up to the wheel where he was crouched down waiting for me. We could barely see each other in the gloom.

‘There’s a boat in the dock. A big one’

‘What? Are you sure?’ it seemed unbelievable. Apart from Jimmy and Mike, we hadn’t seen a single other person back on the mainland and no one knew we were on the island. Whoever it was would have had to get very lucky to come across our island and it made no sense for anyone fleeing from Scotland to be heading north-west rather than north-east to the Shetland islands.

‘It’s there,’ Jake said. ‘I wasn’t sure at first but those rear lights are unmistakable. It’s an old fishing boat. Like a trawler or something.’

'Have they seen us?' I asked, panic beginning to rise in my chest again.

'I don't think so. I killed the engine and the lights as soon as I was sure.'

I thought for a long moment. 'Ok. Let's think about this. They might not be dangerous. They could be friendly. Or if not then very sick. But let's not take any chances.'

'What are you thinking?' Jake asked, still whispering.

Our momentum was carrying us toward the island. If we'd turned the engines back on they'd hear us. We could have driven away from the island, but they'd hear us and be on the alert for our return. We really only had one advantage at that point.

'They can't know how many of us there are. Even if they are known to you, or the others have told them about you and me, they won't know what I look like. If they aren't friendly it would be good to have a surprise up our sleeve.'

Jake was nodding. I continued.

'I think you should go on. Play it innocent when you get there. If they're bad news, you can give me some kind of signal.'

'How will you get back without being seen? Hide in the boat?'

'No. I'll need to slip out before we get too close. I'll swim around the side and try to scale the cliff.' Jake looked uncertain at this. He thought for another crucial moment.

'The water is freezing Carl. Even if you can swim round the side without catching hyperthermia, how are you going to climb the side of the island? It's straight up in most places.'

He had a point. But it was the only way I could think of to stay out of sight.

'I'll wrap my clothes around the gun and use one of those life jackets as a buoy. I'll try and keep them dry. If I can't climb up the side then I'll try to paddle around the shore tomorrow night.' *That might not be soon enough,* I thought. *I have to make that climb somehow.*

'Ok. If you're sure?' I was touched by his genuine concern. I nodded. I snuck a look over the wheel and then returned to crouch by Jake's side.

'There's not much time. What will the signal be? We need something that won't arouse any suspicion'

'I've got a red windbreaker back at the house. I'll hang it in the upstairs window of the big house. If I can't do that I'll find another way to let you know. I'll leave a tool out by the reservoir or get someone else to do it.'

It was a weak plan, but we were running out of time.

'Let's hope it won't be necessary,' I said.

I grabbed one of the life jackets from the side of the boat. It was a bright orange, but still barely visible in the pitch dark of the early hours. Jake disappeared below deck, rummaged around and appeared with what looked like a shiny blanket.

'Fire blanket,' he said. 'Should be water resistant to a degree.'

I stripped down to my underwear and wrapped my clothes around the rifle and then the blanket as tightly as I could around the clothes. The cold air was already enough to make me shiver. Then I tied the lifejacket straps tight around the bundle. It wasn't perfect, but it would have to do.

I looked at Jake and twirled my finger. He understood and fired up the engines.

I moved to the far side of the boat, where I hoped I would be out of view as we headed into the island. I looked once more at Jake, but his vision was dead set on the island. He kept the speed to a medium pace, just as he would if we were approaching under normal circumstances.

With nothing else for it, I slung my bundle over the side of the boat and lowered myself in after it, trying to make as little splash as possible. The cold water ripped the breath from my lungs and it was all I could do just to flap around and keep my head above water.

That kind of freezing temperature is not something the body can acclimatise to. It's not like lowering yourself into a warm bath, or gradually stepping under a cold shower. It puts your body into an inescapable state of shock, making the simplest tasks like breathing, a monumental struggle.

The water was rougher than usual too and I swallowed more than one gulp of the merciless, icy, salt water, as both the boat and my bundle drifted away from me.

I forced myself into a swimming stroke. It was erratic, but the movement helped focus my mind. I reached the bundle and used it to raise my arms out of the water, a small relief. Then I turned and kicked towards the side of the island. I could feel the current dragging me around, so I tried to conserve my energy for when I would need it to break for the shoreline.

With the boat now out ahead of me, there was very little light to guide me in, but the large, dark, mass of land stood out against the cloudy night sky, the darkest shape in a sea of black.

Feeling suddenly and desperately sleepy, I pushed my way to the east side of the island. For several minutes everything faded out of my consciousness except for my rhythmic kicking toward the shore. There was nothing else; no radiation, no strangers, no quest for survival. There was just the kicking of my legs and the tug of the ocean.

And then I was there. Brain clouded and body shaking uncontrollably, I clasped at the sharp rocks which lay at the bottom of the cliff. My hands and feet slipped as I tried to haul myself up and I nearly lost the bundle. In pure animal instinct, I threw the bundle up and out of the water and then clambered after it, opening wounds on my hands and knees which flooded instantly with salt and stung me back to reality.

I perched on a small craggle of rocks by the side of the island. Out of the water but not out of the mind-numbing cold. I fumbled with the bundle, desperate for some warmth. My clothes were dry enough, but my hands were too stiff and numb to get them on, so I simply put them in a pile at my feet and wrapped myself in the blanket. I don't know how long I sat there, a shivering wreck marooned on the unforgiving rocks, but when I finally warmed up enough for rational thought, the first signs of daylight had arrived.

30

Maisie's heart sank when she heard the shot ring out through the dead of night. She hoped it was just a warning shot, but warning or not it meant one thing: the others were back. And it was too soon. She wasn't ready. She hadn't even had the chance to brief the others on her plan.

But she had to do something. This was the moment. This was the chance. And it wouldn't come again.

31

Jake wasn't sure what he would do if they weren't seen. In his head the plan was centred around them being seen cruising into port and then reacting to the situation he encountered. If the newcomers weren't friendly, he was sure he would know about it quickly. If they were then it would be easier. But it was the darkest depths of the morning and if no one heard or saw them, he wasn't sure what the best move would be.

A gunshot woke him out of his thoughts and answered all his questions however. It cracked through the sound of the waves and the engine like a shriek in a crowded market.

He ducked at the sound and glanced around at Jimmy. His eyes were wide open, but he hadn't moved. Jake returned his attention back to the shore and killed the engine. *Not friendly then,* he thought. The reality of it stretched a cold hand up his spine and caused him to shiver. He suddenly felt very cold.

His eyes searched the dark shore for the origin of the shot. He couldn't make out any movement on the shore or the dock. But he could make out the dark flag fluttering at the back of the boat. *It can't be,* he thought. *How?*

The boat continued to drift in towards the shore, propelled by momentum and the tide. After a moment, when no subsequent shot was fired, he felt sure the shot was meant in warning. And this was confirmed when he caught sight of a figure standing at the end of the dock with a long shape held out in front of him, metal gleaming in the light from the boat.

He waited, allowing the boat to continue to drift. When he heard a rustle behind him he raised a palm, to let Jimmy know to stay out of sight. His eyes remained fixed on the man on the dock.

Movement from the corner of his eye broke his gaze and he flicked his eyes to the other boat, which took up most of the space next to the dock. Two other shapes were clambering over the side in a hurry, each with their own shining metal blades in hand. They hit the dock and hurried up to the other man.

Play it innocent, he reminded himself. 'Hello? Steve?' he called out.

The boat's momentum had slowed to a crawl now, but he was only twenty metres or so away.

'Bring it in. Slowly. No funny business.' came the reply.

Jake recognised the voice, confirming his worst fears. He opened the engines up again at their lowest ebb and they kicked into a low growl, like a family dog at the intruders. He did as told and cruised the boat into the dock. As soon as he got there one man grabbed the front and one the back, they began tying the boat away as he killed the engine. The third man, the tallest of the three moved down the dock until he had a clear view (and shot) at Jake. His gun was raised.

'How many aboard skipper?' he asked, with mock gentility.

'Just me and my friend Carl.' He hoped he hadn't put too much emphasis on the name. Just enough to warn Jimmy, but not enough to be noticed by the others.

'Out,' Tim said. 'Nice and slow like'.

Jake raised his hands and nodded his compliance. 'My friend is sick, he'll need my help,' he replied. *I should be asking about the others,* he thought. *Need to show my fear.*

'Make it quick then' was the growled response, followed by a barked order to one of the other men. 'Get up to the house and round them all up.' The man hurried off.

Jake made slow deliberate movements as he lifted Jimmy into a standing position and placed his arm over his shoulder to hold him up. As he did so he asked 'My family, are they…'

'They're fine. For now. But they won't be if you don't get your ass onto this dock sharpish.'

Jake didn't know whether to believe him or not, but felt relieved all the same. He got himself and

Jimmy off the boat and onto the dock as fast as he could.

He stood there in the dim light of both boats, with one man behind him and the other in front. His heart beat hard in his chest, but he tried to remain calm as he made eye contact with the man he had fled from so many months ago.

'Welcome back Jake. Long time no see'. The recognition was mutual.

'Me and the boys here have decided to join you on this little island getaway of yours. Well, I say *yours,* it's *ours* now, isn't it Greig?'

Behind him, Greig forced a chuckle.

'We'll do whatever you say Tim,' Jake said. 'Please just don't hurt my family.'

It's all down to you now Carl, he thought. But he was wrong about that.

32

I dressed myself slowly, my numb, swollen fingers and fatigued brain fumbling through the task. The fire blanket had done its job. My clothes were damp in some places, but they were dry enough. Once I was clothed, I wrapped myself in the blanket again and huddled back down on the rock, trying my best to warm up and kick start my body into action.

I needed a plan. I knew the first step was to climb the cliff face and get to the top of the island. But then what? The grey light of dawn was swiftly turning into the full light of morning and despite the overcast gloom, I would still be easy to spot. A lone figure against the backdrop of the greens and greys of the island.

I tried to picture the view from the big house; what could and couldn't be seen from the windows and surrounding area. If Jake had done his part and the others had followed suit, then the invaders wouldn't have any idea that I was there. Would they post sentries anyway? I doubted it. But I would still need to be careful.

The shortest part of the cliff was in front of me. I would be out of sight during the climb, but at the top I would be in full sight of the boats and the shore. If I stayed very low and quiet I could crawl up and away from the shoreline and out of sight from the houses, but that would be the most risky part. So before I clambered over the summit I would have to peer over the surface and make sure no one was in easy view.

A wave crashed hard against the rocks, spraying cold water over me. I realised that all I was really doing was putting off the crux of the matter - climbing up the slippery rocks of the cliff. If I couldn't do that, then none of the rest mattered.

I glanced up at the wall in front of me. It was a mixture of light and dark greys, punctuated here and there with splotches of green. I would have to avoid those mossy areas as much as possible. The surfaces would be slippery enough from the sea spray, without adding damp moss into the equation. I noticed that the rocks towards the top of the cliff were a lighter colour than those at the bottom, which was likely to mean they were dryer, being so much further from the sea. The rocks at the bottom also looked angrier, with more jagged edges striking out into the air. These ledges would be helpful in the first phase of the climb, but after that the difficulty of the slippery rocks would be replaced by that of the smoother ones.

A shot rang out from the other side of the island, cracking through the regular hiss and smash of the sea. Like the starting gun of a race, it sprung me into action. I slung the rifle over my head and made for the base of the cliff, my head full of adrenaline and ice-cold fear. *Oh God, don't let me be too late. Please don't let me be too late.*

33

Having been marched at gunpoint up the slope to the Big House, Jake was relieved to find his children alive and well. As well as they could be anyway.

He'd been ordered into the front room, where Susan, Steve and the kids had been rounded up and forced to wait. They didn't move when he appeared, but their eyes were wide and focused on him as he stumbled through the door with Jimmy propped up against him.

'Daddy!' Aileen cried out.

'Can you help me with Carl?' Jake asked quickly. 'He's sick, but ok.' He looked hard at Susan and Steve, his voice deliberate. Then he looked at the kids and made a silent shushing motion with his lips. His back was to the invaders and he hoped the others could read the explanation on his face.

While Susan and Steve seemed to understand, he was pretty sure the kids wouldn't. He prayed they would do as he said and keep quiet, until he had the chance to explain it to them.

Susan took the bait. 'Oh Carl, you poor thing,' she said, as she rose to help Jake lay Jimmy down. She fussed over him, giving Jake a chance to move over to the kids and hold them close. He whispered to them as Susan covered for him with loud questions to Jimmy.

'It's Susan, Carl. Do you recognise me? Are you hurt anywhere?'

Steve played his part too, standing and distracting Tim and the others as they followed Jake into the room.

'Can Karen join us?' he asked, palms held up ahead of him in supplication. 'She'll be worried about him.'

'Karen's busy. Now get back down,' Tim commanded. He surveyed the room. Jake held the children close, Susan held the back of her hand against Jimmy's head and Steve resumed his seat on the floor. Tim's eyes went wide.

'Where is she?' he demanded, his voice rising.

The others looked at him blankly. He turned to Paul.

'I told you to round them up. Where's Maisie?'

Paul shrugged. 'Couldn't find her boss. Figured it best to wait for you.'

Tim shook his head in frustration before turning to Greig. 'Have a look will you? This idiot probably missed her,' he ordered.

Greig tore up the stairs. There were fast

footsteps all around the ceiling, as he checked the other rooms, before coming crashing back down the stairs and sprinting through the downstairs areas and out to the kitchen. When he returned his face was white.

'She's not here,' he said, in a weak voice.

Up until this point Tim felt that he had asserted his dominance over the islanders well and they had followed his instructions to the letter. Now, in the early hours of daybreak, Maisie had disappeared while they were distracted dragging Jake back from the shore. He was furious that he'd let his guard down.

'Stay here and watch them,' he ordered Paul, before turning to the Greig. 'You, wait out front for me. And keep your eyes peeled.'

He left the room, slamming the door behind him and headed upstairs.

Karen heard him coming from her post in the room with the sick man. She crouched over him and grabbed his wrist, a position she hoped looked like she was doing her best to care for Alan. Tim burst into the room, but her quick thinking seemed to work and his approach softened when he saw her.

'Where's Maisie?' he asked, fierce but restrained.

'I don't know,' she replied. 'I've been here, just as you said.'

It was the truth and he could sense that. He hesitated a moment, keen to ask about his brother but reluctant to show any hint of concern or weakness.

'He's stable,' she said, anticipating his

question.

'He better be.' the hardness returned to his voice. He walked over to Alan, forcing Karen out of the way. He peered down at his brother and placed a hand on his shoulder. Alan groaned in recognition.

'You alright Alan?' he said. Alan didn't reply. But he was visibly breathing and looked more comfortable than he had before they arrived at the island.

Tim stood up and looked around the room, his eyes settling on Karen who was now sprawled against the far side of the room.

'You have everything you need?' he asked her.

'Yes. Yes, I think so.' And then with some courage, 'I could use a break. Something to eat maybe?'

'Fine,' he said. 'You can join the others downstairs. I'll bring you something. Ten minutes and then I want you back up here.'

'Thank you,' she said, surprised but genuinely grateful. She followed him downstairs and joined the others in the front room while he went to the kitchen.

Her strength failed her when she saw Jake and she flung herself into his arms, tears streaming down her face.

'I'm sorry,' she cried.

Jake pulled away from her and put his hand under her chin, guiding her eyes to his. He spoke deliberately.

'It's ok. Carl is sick,' he said and motioned

towards Jimmy. 'He made it back, but he's not in good health. He'll need your help.' Jake stared hard at her, until he saw the understanding creep into her face. She nodded and went over to Jimmy, checking him over with her soft, professional touch.

Tim returned with a bowl of raw, roughly cut vegetables which he forced into her hands.

'Eat he said. Then I want you back upstairs. The rest of you stay here. And you better hope we find Maisie.'

He stormed out, leaving them under the glare of Paul.

'Any sign of her?' he asked, joining Greig outside. The other man shook his head.

Tim glanced around the horizon in the grey light of morning, his face darkening further. With a sudden movement he whipped his shotgun into the air and fired at the sky.

'Maisie!' he yelled. 'You better get your fine arse back here or these kids will face the consequences!'

He stood silent for a few minutes, listening for footsteps or any other sign of response. Not getting one, he turned to Greig, his face full of threat and malice.

'Go find her,' he ordered. 'If you're not back here in 30 minutes then so help me…' he didn't need to finish the warning. Greig turned quickly and made to head up the island, pausing only to hear Tim's last instruction.

'I want her alive,' he said. 'It's time she learned

some obedience the hard way. From all of us'

Greig nodded, a smile touching his lips.

34

From her position just inside the entrance of the dome, Maisie heard the shot and could just about make out Tim's words over the ever-present noise of the sea. She looked down at the shovel in her hand. She still didn't know what her plan was, but she knew that going back right now was the wrong decision. She lowered herself to a crouch and made her way out and up towards the reservoir.

35

I almost slipped immediately, as I rushed across the rocks to the foot of the cliff, my boots sliding on the slimy surface. Fortunately I skidded towards the cliff face and not backwards. My body slammed into the wall in front of me, my outflung hands gripping anything they could latch on to to keep me upright. It was a harsh reminder of how easy it would be to twist an ankle and ruin any chance I had of scaling the cliff and rescuing the others. At that height at least a fall would be survivable. But any higher up and it would be lethal.

I steadied my breathing and tried to remember my training. It was so many years ago and it was the last time I had attempted to climb anything at all.

I looked up into the dim light and tried to plot my course. *Keep it simple,* I thought. *One foothold at a time. Steady yourself. Look for the next one.*

I tried to push the gunshot out of my mind. There hadn't been another one. So at the very least, *some* of my friends were still alive. As much as I wanted to rush, the best way I could help them was to make sure I scaled the damn cliff safely.

With my first few holds planned, I tentatively lifted myself up, placing my right foot on a jut of sharp rock and reaching up with my left hand for support. I lifted my left foot next, to another small ledge, about a foot higher up. Lifted with my right hand. Stopped. Breathed. Checked my balance and moved onto the next.

The rock was slippery, but down here the hand and foot holds were pronounced and obvious. Taking it slow and testing my grip, I surmounted the first eight foot comfortably. The rock above this level was lighter in colour and less damp then at the bottom, but still not dry enough to provide any confidence. Twice my left hand slipped from a hold milliseconds before I attempted to lift myself. On both occasions my heart, already beating hard, felt like it would burst through my ribs. I paused and fought hard against the rising panic. *Breath. Compose. Plan the next step.*

After the second time, when reaching up with my left hand and applying pressure I felt a sharp pain in my palm. I brought my hand down in front of my face and saw that it had been cut in several places. Not deep enough to cause serious damage, but enough that the salt and pressure hurt like hell.

I looked down. Mistake. Although I was only a third of the way up the cliff, it was high enough to trigger a vertigo which froze me in place for several minutes. I gripped hard against the wall, pain in my hand forgotten.

Breathe. Compose. Plan. My mantra brought me back to the task at hand.

I could hear birds above me, squawking their daily greeting to the sun. Another thing I would have to be wary of. One panicked petrel could surprise me and send me crashing back to the rocks below in a flash of feathers and fear.

I continued upwards. Halfway up and the holds were becoming less obvious. But they were there and though I sometimes had to stretch further to reach them, they were less slippery to the touch. I became skilled at detecting moss on an unseen jut of rock, the spongy surface giving it away. More than once I decided to look for a different hold, rather than risk one with a dose of the soft green plant.

The birds were louder now. Whether that was because I was closer to them, or because they had detected my presence and were warning me off, I couldn't be sure. *Expect the surprise,* I tried to tell myself. *Let it happen. Don't react.*

It happened sooner than I'd expected. Reaching up to what looked like a decent sized crease in the cliff, my fingers plunged into something brittle and sharp, a thousand tiny, fragile needles. There was a cacophony of small squawks and something bounced off my head. And then again off my shoulder. I jerked my hand out and with it came a small nest of some kind, its contents spilling down to the water far below. The nest remained attached to my fingers and as I shook my hand hard on pure instinct, my foot slipped out from beneath me.

Adrenaline shot through my body and I flailed

out, smashing the nest into pieces as my hand desperately sought out a hold. It couldn't find one and as I swung about on the cliff my other foot slid out. I looked up in panic at my sole remaining hold as my feet scrabbled for purchase beneath me. It was my left hand, bent at the knuckles and bleached white from the strain, gripped to a ledge no wider than four fingers. Whether from the weight of my body, the slipperiness of the surface or the blood on my hand from the cuts, I felt it slowly slipping.

36

Maisie watched as the man walked around the circumference of the reservoir, looking up and around the island as he went. She had the perfect vantage point and was grateful she had continued right to the top of the highest point of the island, rather than waiting further down. She had pulled herself up onto the flat surface of the peak and laid flat on her stomach, out of sight except for her forehead and eyes, which focused intently on the invader below.

Although the back of the left hand side of the island was steep and easily visible from most places around the reservoir, there were several large boulders and outcrops of earth above, which could keep a person out of sight from someone below them. The man was clearly conscious of this, creeping up to one at a time and then swinging himself around the side, gun held at the ready.

After circumventing the reservoir and taking stock of what (he thought) was every hiding place on that side of the island, he began making his way off to the right. He continued systematically checking any other potential hiding places as he went. When he was nearly out of sight in the gloom, Maisie considered her options. She was well hidden up on the shelf, but her only advantage would come from surprise. She knew she would only have one chance of taking the man out - catching him off guard with a hard swing of the shovel to his head. But she couldn't do that from where she was. However, if she followed him and he heard her, she would be out of range and in the open. And his gun would make short work of her.

She still hadn't made up her mind as the man disappeared from view.

37

I had one thought as my hand slipped from the rock. *Hit the water, not the rocks.*

I made to swing my feet underneath me, intending to kick out hard from the cliff face and launch myself outwards, away from the rocks below. But as my fingers slipped clear from the ledge, my right foot found a hard surface and my right hand, flung hard at the cliff in desperation, caught hold of the side of an outcrop. The momentum swung me out to the right, loosening the grip of my hand. My right shoulder smashed into the wall and I lost hold of the outcrop, my body sliding downwards and my foot pivoting upwards, toes first away from the surface. I felt myself fall.

For the briefest of moments, my mind went blank. It took me a second to realise I had only fallen a couple of inches and something was pressing hard against my chest. My heel was still pressed into the ledge, but not enough to keep me upright. I looked at my chest and saw the strap of the rifle, dug deep into my body, holding me in place. The metal link between the strap and the top of the rifle had caught on a jagged piece of rock and held me suspended in the air. If my right foot had slipped all the way, my weight would have been enough to break the strap and send me sprawling to my death, but somehow I had just enough purchase with my foot to counter balance it.

Instinct kicked in, driving my movements without conscious thought. I swung my left hand around to the other side of the outcrop and pulled myself around just far enough to regain purchase with my right foot. My hand screamed in pain, but my scattered brain ignored it. I lifted my left knee and scrabbled for a foot hold. Finding one, I was finally able to free my right arm from against the cliff and turn myself fully flat against the surface, face first. I balanced myself with my right hand and closed my eyes. Adrenaline surged through me until I was shivered.

Breathe. Compose. Plan.

It took me several minutes, but eventually calm returned. With some effort, I lifted my head and opened my eyes. I could see what looked like a good hold above me, but it would mean moving - and having found a position of safety, my body was refusing to budge.

I counted off in my head three times, practicing the move in my head. *Three, two, one, go.*

On the forth count I finally fired my brain into motion, reaching out and securing my grip. My eyes locked on the top of the cliff. It seemed so close, but still impossibly far away.

Filled with fear, panic and adrenaline, every move was hard. But the only way out now was upwards.

Breathe. Compose. Plan.

The noise of the ocean, the squawk of the birds and the pain of the scratches and cuts on my body, all fell away. They were replaced by the singular focus on continuing upwards, one hold at a time. So deep and hard was my concentration that I almost didn't realise it, when the next obvious hold was the top of the cliff and survival from the climb.

Spurred on by the sudden realisation that I'd made it and my desperation to be safe, I launched my hand upward, gripped the soggy ground and let out a gasp of victory.

'Who the hell are you?'

There was a shape above me. A person I didn't recognise. And a shotgun pointed at my head.

38

‘What’s taking him so long?’ Tim demanded out loud, to no one in particular. He was stood outside the front door of the big house, glancing around the back of the island. Something caught his eye off to the far right, where the shoreline met a wall of rock which rose up to the cliffs and formed the right side of the island.

He saw a figure, stood bolt upright and peering over the edge of the cliff. Another figure appeared behind him, smaller and moving quickly. The taller figure turned slightly, as if he’d been alerted to a sound behind him. But before he had the chance to turn fully around, the smaller figure struck him hard across the face with something almost the height of their waist.

The taller figure crumbled under the weight of the blow, pitching out and over the cliff edge. It happened in a flash and the man was gone.

‘That fucking bitch,’ Tim said. He turned back to the big house and stormed through the door, yelling out to his companion.

Behind him the smaller figure reached down and hauled something over the side of the cliff.

39

'Maisie!' I cried out.

She looked over the cliff edge and stared at me in shock. Her relief and disgust at pitching Greig over the side to his death was replaced by wild surprise.

'Carl?' she asked in disbelief.

'Can you help me?' I asked, my pain and panic running away at the sight of her.

She reached down and grabbed my arm under the shoulder. I pushed up with my tired legs and grasped the summit with my other hand. Together we hauled my body up and over onto the cold, damp ground. Relief swept through me. And with it, a deep fatigue and ache in every muscle. I lay there for a moment, face pressed into the sweet smelling grass of my island.

'We've got to get moving Carl…Vasiliy. Whatever your name is. They could spot us from here.'

I felt the sting of her comment worse than the

pain in my hand and the scrapes on the rest of my body. She had neither forgotten nor forgiven. And she was still uncertain about me.

I stood up slowly. By the time I was fully upright, she was already on her way up the back of the island. I followed as quickly as I could manage, with a limp in my step. We reached the back of the island, but Maisie didn't stop. She kept going at a fast pace, until we were all the way up just below the peak.

'I've got an idea but we'll have to be quick. They'll be coming for us. How far can you shoot that thing?' she gestured to my rifle.

'It's been a long time since I last had any target practice. I think about 20 feet, if we need to be certain of any accuracy.'

She thought for a beat.

'It'll need to be further than that. You don't have to kill with the shot, you just have to hit.'

'What's the plan?'

She explained it to me quickly. I had my doubts, but we were out of time.

40

The others could see Tim was furious as soon as he flew into the room.

'Go get the other one,' he growled at Paul and then raised his gun and aimed it at Jake. Paul hurried upstairs to bring Karen back down to the living room for the second time.

'Your daughter is going to come and help us find that bitch sister-in-law of yours. The rest of you are going to sit right here and not move a fucking muscle or it'll be this little one's last day on the island.'

'No Tim, please, you don't need her. I'll come with you. I won't be any trouble,' Jake pleaded.

Tim stormed across the room and smashed the butt of his shotgun in Jake's head, throwing him onto his back. The kids screamed and Susan hurried to them.

'This isn't open for discussion. I've played nice until now, but Maisie has decided to ruin it for all of you. Now you're going to do exactly as I say or I'm going to start shooting.'

Paul returned, dragging Karen behind him. He tossed her onto the floor next to Steve.

'What's going on?' she asked, her voice trembling.

'Back against the wall, all of you!' Tim shouted.

Susan helped Jake up, Steve helped Jimmy and Karen pulled the kids back with her. They were crying and shaking with fear.

'Get some rope or string or something. Anything you can find,' Tim said to Paul. Paul left the room to carry out the order. The others could sense that he was almost as scared as they were.

Tim knelt a few feet away from Karen and the kids, gun trained on them. He spoke to Aileen.

'What's your name sweetheart?'

'Leave her alone!' Karen cried. Tim fired a deafening shot into the wall of the house, sending small pieces of the brickwork flying. The others pressed themselves into the wall, covering their heads to shield against the blast.

In one stride Tim covered the distance between them and grabbed Aileen's arm, ripping her free from her mother's grasp. She screamed and flailed about, but he held her firm.

'Tim, please! There's no need for this,' Jake said. 'We'll do whatever you say!'

Tim pointed his gun at Jake but spoke to Karen.

'Calm her down Karen. She's coming with us

and I can't have her crying and hollering like this. She won't be hurt as long as Maisie quits playing her games.'

Karen crept over to Aileen and took her hand. Tim kept his gun pointed at Jake.

'It's ok sweetie, everything's all right,' she said through tears. 'I need you to be brave now ok. If you be brave, the man won't shoot his gun anymore. Will you?' she looked up at Tim, begging him.

Tim softened his voice, but the fire was still there.

'That's right darlin'. We're just going for a little walk, you and me. I need you to help me find Maisie.'

Aileen's whimpering tempered down to a sniffle.

'I don't want to,' she said. 'Mummy, I don't want to!'

'You've got to Aileen. Maisie is missing and you've got to go and find her. We need to stay here in case she comes back, right?' she looked up at Tim again.

'That's right. You come with us and be a good girl and everyone will be ok. You understand?'

Aileen looked at Karen. She seemed to recognise the pleading in her mother's face and knew this was one of those times when it was best not to test her. Her mother looked sad, not angry. Perhaps it was best to do as she said. She nodded once and stared at the ground.

'Good girl,' Karen said, the gratitude clear in

her voice. 'Good girl Aileen. Everything will be alright, you'll see.'

'Don't hurt her Tim. Please.' Jake begged one last time.

'She'll be fine,' Tim said. 'I can't promise the same for the rest of you if you don't shut up and do as I say though.' They didn't need another warning.

Paul returned carrying a mix of electrical cables and scarves.

'All I could find,' he said, and then waited for further instruction.

'Tie 'em up. Tie 'em to each other if you can,' Tim said. 'And don't try anything you lot. Once this one's done with, I can always take the young lad over there.' He motioned towards Tom with his gun and then lowered it to hover just above Aileen's head.

Paul went to work tying the others up, one by one. He used the electrical cable to tie their wrists behind their back, pulling them so tight they gasped. Then he used the scarves as rope to tie them to each other. It was ramshackle work, but it would be effective for a while at least.

Once he was done, he returned to his leader's side. Tim glanced around at them one by one, forcing them to stare at the ground under the weight of his glare.

'Not one move until we get back,' he said and stormed out of the room, dragging Aileen with him. His lackey followed right behind him.

41

From my place laid flat on the top of the island's summit, I saw them coming. Well, I heard them first, then I saw them.

The leader was singing something in a high growl, to the tune of the old song Daisy Bell. As they came closer I could make out the words.

'Maisie, Maisie where the hell are you?' He sang the same line over and over, as he and his companion made their slow way up the back of the island. There was a sinister smile on his face, but his glance swung from left to right, giving away how intent he was on the task at hand.

As he came around the near side of the reservoir, I saw Aileen with him, her wrist held tight in his hand. It was a disaster.

Maisie's plan had been centred around them coming to look for us, which she knew they'd have to do at some point. Whether they came together or alone was of no consequence, but we hadn't banked on them bringing a hostage. That changed everything.

But it was too late now. Maisie was in her hiding place behind a boulder high up near the ridge on the back of the island. She was out of sight and had no way of knowing Aileen was with them. I could only hope they would give it away somehow. The surprise of seeing Aileen with them could ruin the only advantage we would have. And I was already unsure of the shot, without the potential of missing and hitting the little girl.

The leader had sent the other invader around the far side of the reservoir to look for Maisie. With neither of them finding anything in any of the possible hiding places on either side, they rejoined above the water.

They looked uncertain as to their next move. The leader looked from right to left, trying to decide which way to go next. After some hushed conversation, the other man moved down to the side of the reservoir and stood there facing the right hand side of the island. Then the leader headed further up the island, dragging the little girl with him.

They don't want us cutting back in behind them and getting back to the others, I thought. *They must have checked the shore and outbuildings already.*

I tightened my grip around the rifle. *This might still work.* It was more of a prayer than a conscious thought.

The leader continued to search, swinging this way and that as he made his way up the back of the island. He was growing increasingly impatient and had stopped singing altogether. Finally, about fifteen foot away from Maisie's hiding place, he lost it altogether.

'Maisie!' he shouted out. 'Enough of this! I have your little niece here with me. Show yourself or she'll be the loser of your little game!'

Yes! I thought. That gives us a chance. I focused on taking aim for my shot. Maisie's voice ran through my head *'It doesn't have to kill him. It just has to hit him.'*

I lowered the sight until it was aimed square between his shoulder blades. If I missed high or low, I would still hit him.

Maisie came out of hiding, holding her shovel in one hand and her palm up with her other.

'I'm here. Let her go, it's me you want'

'Maisie!' he cried, as if meeting a long lost friend in a foreign city. 'Nice of you to make an appearance.'

'Let her go,' Maisie said again. 'Send her back to the house. We can sort this out between us.'

'There's nothing to sort out Maisie. You killed my man and disobeyed my instructions. The only choice you have now is how bad your punishment will be. And that depends very much on how hard you make this.' He had his gun trained on her. Aileen had begun crying again.

Maisie dropped the shovel in front of her and got down on her knees, her hands held up.

'What do you want me to do Tim?' she asked.

His name was the signal. I checked my aim,

exhaled, held my breath and squeezed the trigger.

A crack echoed out around the top of the island. Tim spun around at the sound, just in time to see his companion fall forward onto his face, a bullet wound in his back.

That split second was all the time Maisie needed. She was up and running, grabbing the shovel as she went.

I swung the rifle around, trying to take aim at Tim in case she didn't make it.

'Run Aileen!' I yelled at the top of my lungs, if only to confuse him further and buy Maisie a second more. It worked and he spun around the opposite direction, to the sound of my voice. He must have seen her out of the corner of his eye though and he did a double take just in time to see the shovel crash into the side of his face. It broke off at the handle, weakening the full power of the swing, but it was enough to make him stumble forwards and release Aileen from his grasp.

Aileen ran down the hill and I jumped up and over the summit. But my fatigued legs gave way underneath me and instead of jumping into a crouching run, I crashed into the ground below. I grasped at the rifle, trying to take aim.

Tim wasn't down yet, but he had dropped his gun and stumbled forwards, away from Maisie. She dropped the broken shovel and ran at him lunging at his back and with a shove, to keep him off balance. He fell forwards, his hands just stopping him from hurtling over the side.

'Maisie!' I yelled. She had begun to charge again, but he was recovering and I was desperate to keep some space between them. She heard and stopped, swinging her head round in my direction. She saw the muzzle aimed at Tim and stepped back. I waited until he regained his feet and fired.

I missed this time, but it was enough to make him duck. It was only for a second, a reaction to the loud bang from the gun, but it was long enough again for Maisie to finish the job. She charged, her hands making contact with his right shoulder and tipping him over the edge. She almost fell with him, her momentum carrying her towards the cliff, but she went to the ground at waist height and caught herself, hands spread wide on the cliff face beneath her.

It was near to the highest place on the island and we had time to hear him yell and see the birds nearby take flight in surprise, before he hit the rocks below with a sickening, wet thump.

I raced over to Maisie and helped her up. Her eyes were fixed on the spot where she'd pushed him over.

'Maisie,' I said, placing my hand gently on the side of her face and turning her eyes towards mine. 'It's over.'

We stared at each other. After a second she reached out and pulled me close and we stood like that, holding each other for dear life, on the very edge of the world.

I could have stood like that forever, but after a mere moment she released me and without saying a word, turned and headed back down towards the village. I stood staring after her.

When she got to the body of the other man she kicked it hard. Nothing. He was gone. She began to try and drag him up the island by one arm, but was as weakened as I was from the exertion of the last few hours. I hurried down the hill to help her.

We dragged him up the hill slowly, gasping from the effort, and tossed him over the side. I watched him go, as Maisie turned and headed back down the hillside again.

We had won, but it was evident that my own battle was not yet over. I still had some explaining to do.

42

We all sat around the kitchen table in the big house, staring at the floor and waiting for Karen and Maisie to return. They had taken the kids upstairs. They were exhausted but hysterical and it took some time to calm them down and convince them that the bad men were gone.

Maisie had asked us to wait in the kitchen. She said she had something we needed to discuss. The others were confused. Only I knew what that was likely to be. The wait was agony, but both my body and mind were glad to be still and silent for a while.

Finally they returned, having gotten the kids to sleep. Karen took a seat next to Jake and took his hand. There was an empty seat next to me, but Maisie ignored it, instead standing against the far wall.

Steve looked at her and then back at me. He wasn't sure what to make of it. Jake and Karen were focused on each other. It was Susan who broke the silence.

'Maisie?' she asked.

'Carl...' she stopped herself. 'Vasili here has something he wants to tell us.'

Jake looked up, confusion written large across his weary face.

'Vasili? Who's Vasili?' he asked.

'Me,' I said. 'Vasili is my real name, not Carl. I told Maisie the night we left the island.'

'Vasili?' Steve said and then the realisation hit him.

One by one around the table, a stunned understanding struck their faces. None of them got as far as Maisie had done in the moment I'd told her, but they realised enough. I could feel the sense of betrayal emanating from them. And it was devastating.

'You're…?' Susan asked

'Russian, yes.' I said.

We sat in silence for a minute. I could see the others turning their thoughts over in their heads. There was nothing for it. If they were ever to understand, they would have to hear the full story.

'I was an orphan,' I began. The first and last time I would ever tell the story.

43

‘I was born in Novosibirsk and raised in an orphanage on the outskirts of the city. When I was old enough, I was told that my father had left shortly before I was born and that my mother died in childbirth. The state had tried to reach my father, but he was long gone and I had no living relatives that could be found. So I was sent to the orphanage.

It wasn’t so bad. There were lots of other boys like me and we were treated well. Except for our circumstances, we grew up like any other children. We went to school, we played, we were obedient and disobedient in equal measures.’

I shrugged my shoulders to emphasise that this was no big deal. Not perfect, but not terrible either. The others made no response, they just continued to stare at me. So I took a sip of water and continued.

‘Up until my early teenage years my education was the same as any other child. Maths, Sciences,

Geography and the rest. But then things changed. Our lessons began to focus more on technology and physical education took on a more military nature. We were taught how to run and climb and shoot.

You must understand that I had no idea until I got older, that this was different to other children. As a teenage boy I thought it was wonderful, learning about weapons and playing war games with my friends. I enjoyed the computer studies too and had quite the aptitude for it. We didn't realise it at the time, but we were being given access to the latest technology and being taught how to use it. For good and for ill.

When I reached the age of sixteen I was brought before a panel of men dressed in military uniform. They asked me lots of questions, like how I felt about the way the State had provided for me and which of my studies I enjoyed the most. It seemed to go on for hours and oftentimes I felt like I was saying the same things over and over again: I was happy with my education and grateful that I had been so well cared for and got to use computers and shoot guns.

When it was finally over one of the men stood up and came over to me, placing his hand on my shoulder.

"You are a good young man," he said. "But now *we* need *your* help. If you come with us, you will have the opportunity to repay the State for the care it has provided you."

It didn't occur to me at the time what he meant, or that he wasn't actually *asking* me. I think I may have asked him if I could still learn computers and do target practice. I still wasn't sure what was going on.

I agreed and that very afternoon I went with them all the way to Moscow, to a beautiful facility the likes of which I couldn't ever have imagined. I had travelled with them alone and was filled with wonder and gratitude to these men who had chosen me.

Over the next two years it became clear that I was being trained to be a spy. In addition to computer science and physical training, I was taught English every day. Me and the others were told to speak English only, even to each other during our down time. We were constantly corrected on our grammar and pronunciation. By the time of my eighteenth birthday my English was almost perfect.

I was given a back story and sent to attend university in London. I was to be just another British student, a bit of a geek even, with a love of computers. The importance of never revealing my true identity was ingrained into me. I was encouraged to make friends, but keep them distant and focus on my school work.

When I graduated I was told to look for a job in IT security. Any job, as long as it helped me to use and strengthen my computer skills in practice. I still hadn't been tasked with anything covert and considered myself to be living a normal life. I never returned to Russia in all that time, not even once. My only contact came via a laptop which was delivered to me by hand and replaced every few months. The old ones were sent back, in the same box the new one had arrived in.

After several years building a good CV in the

IT industry I received instruction to start looking for any available jobs at a list of certain companies. Which I did. And with my skills and CV, I secured one without too much effort.

It occurred to me that I was probably being placed as a sleeper. Someone who could compromise the security of an organisation from the inside, if ever required to. But I was *never* asked to. I continued to work and live as any other person, right up until the attack.'

I sat back and took another sip of water. I wondered if I had put too much emphasis on never doing any actual espionage. It was true, but I was so desperate to make that point to them that I might have sounded overly zealous. I didn't want to lose the only real friends I had ever had.

Jake confirmed my worst fears - they were struggling to believe me.

'You don't have to lie to us Carl...er, *Vasili*,' Jake said. 'If you did any covert work, it really doesn't matter now.'

'It doesn't make any sense,' said Steve, shaking his head. 'Why would they put all that effort into training you, only to not use you when you were on the inside?'

I looked at Maisie. She turned her eyes to the window and said nothing.

I sighed.

'I can't tell you why, because I don't know. I can tell you that all nations do these things. There are spies from every country, in every country. Even when they are allies. More often than not I think it is because of some foolish sense of needing to be prepared. To not be caught off guard. Or to not have the other team know more than you'

'I see,' said Jake. 'Please go on.'

'So as I said, I was never asked to do anything covert, despite my many years undercover. I had even begun to think that perhaps they had forgotten about me. But every now and then I would receive a message on one of the laptops, asking for my status and general well being. And that reminded me who I really was.'

I gulped down the rest of the water and put the glass down on the table. The next bit would be the hardest.

'I knew about the attack. I cannot lie about that. If I hadn't, I never would have made it to this island.' I said.

There was a collective gasp from the others in the room. All apart from Maisie, who knew already. She continued to stare out the window and my heart ached at the coolness in her eyes.

'Why didn't you try to warn anyone?' Susan asked. There was an accusation in her voice. I had no right to expect anything else.

'I *did* try. I promise you I did. I received a generic message 48 hours before the first missile was fired. It was just two lines, probably sent to every spy all over the world. "All personnel are to return to Russia immediately by any means possible, avoiding major cities. This is not a drill." I knew what that meant: a potential preemptive strike. The man who could not afford to back-down was being forced to. So he would seek to kill millions, rather than risk his authority being questioned. The end of everything, to satisfy one man's ego.

If Nuclear war was upon us, I had no intention of returning to a debriefing room in Moscow as the missiles rained down. I knew it meant total destruction on a global scale, so I chose to run. But as I fled, I made countless calls to all the major British news outlets and tried to warn them of the imminent attack. But they all ignored me. They thought I was playing some kind of game. I don't think anybody, myself included to some extent, really thought this could ever happen.

Even as I sat in my car that night, ready to flee the mainland, I still didn't *really* believe it. How could we reach this point? How could anyone allow this to happen? But we had and it did.'

We all sat in silence, remembering that awful night and the subsequent fallout. Steve got up to refill our glasses. Then he sat back down and resumed staring at the table in front of him. I didn't know what to say next. There was so much they could never understand. So much that even I didn't understand. How could I ever begin to explain it to them?

Jake, his old face battle worn from the struggles of the last few months, but still as composed and dignified as ever, took the lead again.

'Why,' he began, and then paused, considering his words. 'I understand the ultimatum, but politicians are often tight on answers and loose on rhetoric. I assume no global leader can fire a nuclear warhead by themselves. So what do you think actually led to the first missile being fired?'

I shook my head. I had no answers for them, I could only speculate.

'Maybe it was a mistake. A system failure, a breach of protocol, a falling satellite that triggered an early warning system,' I said. 'Simply by being on the edge of global war, we were at risk of destruction from a dose of paranoia and a computer glitch. But *why* the missiles were fired is the wrong question. A historian would tell us that it is not the *why* that explains what happened in the past, so much as the *how*. How did this happen? How did the world reach this point? '

I braced myself. Attempting to explain the world as I saw it without sparking outrage or accusations of misguided sympathies would be no mean feat.

'If we are assigning blame then we need look no further than the leader who ordered the aggression. That much is obvious. No act of aggression is compulsory, no matter what the factors at play. The man who chooses to act in aggression, is the person responsible for the result of that action. No amount of back and forth over what came before is relevant. There is always a choice *not* to kill.

But leaders are not the sole owners of the blame. There is a special place in hell reserved for those who follow murderous orders without question - politicians who value their own ambitions over morality and the sanctity of life. Generals of vast armies who know better than all of us what is and isn't a defensive action, yet still carry out orders of aggression given to them by small men sat behind big desks.

Blame tells us nothing useful though. The world has seen men like these before, over all the ages of humankind. Unless we seek to understand *how* they get to such positions of absolute power, we will never learn how to stop them before it's too late.

The two most powerful and ruinous dictators of the last century came to power through democratic means. They then consolidated their power through a gradual chipping away of the checks and balances of democracy and freedom of expression.

When we look back at this we again ask *why?* Why did your average person first elect and then tolerate these burgeoning dictatorships? The answer lies in fear and division. You do not need to fight the people with guns to get control of them. You simply need to convince them that the people without guns want to take them and that only you can stop them. Or you can impoverish them - use policies to subtly channel all the money to a small elite, while making an average person fearful and desperate. Then convince them another group is to blame for their destitution, but you are their saviour. Divide and conquer, it is the oldest tactic in the book.

But what could be used to scare Russians?

What 'The West' never understood about the Russian mentality is that it is steeped in a deep desire to always be prepared for the worst. As a result, the motivation behind Russian action is not always what you may think it is. We are a nation of many borders that has seen endless conflict throughout the ages. We have been attacked and betrayed time and again for centuries and that has given us a deep desire to appear strong and always be ready to act if we have to. But believe me, along with that desire to appear strong and therefore discourage aggression, is a long lasting desire for peace.

For example, everyone assumes that Russia's alliance with China had roots in an appreciation for dictatorial communist regimes. But consider the geography: a strong alliance with China secures an enormous stretch of Russia's south eastern border and a strong Chinese government maintains peace in that area so that Russia doesn't have to.

The civil war in Syria is another example. When the US did not intervene, Russia saw it as a global duty to bring about stability in the region, and in doing, protect its not too distant borders. In that conflict Russia picked the side of our historical alliance, yes, but we also thought it was the side most likely to win quickly and bring stability back to the region.

This global intervention was not new. It was Russia that defeated Napoleon. And Churchill himself said that "the Red Army tore the guts out of the German war machine" in the second World War. These victories form the fabric of our national identity: a strong nation that has saved the world from evil, but is neither trusted nor respected on the global scene. The Russian conscience struggles to understand the reasons for that.

You see, the Russian people feel that when the world needs Russia, Russia is there. But when it doesn't, Russia is feared, vilified and disregarded. Because of this it is easy for us to believe it when we are told that the nation is once again under threat. I do not seek to justify that mindset, only to try and explain it.

Because of this long history, when our leadership tells us that the West does not intend for us to follow our own path, we are easily convinced. We believe it is important to be strong for our own safety. But also, and believe me this is true my friends: we believe it is our nation's duty to be ready, should we ever be needed again for global stability.

Aggressive actions and cheating in sports, although wrong, come from the same place. They are driven by the desire to win at any cost and be recognised as a great nation of the world - again, to discourage aggression toward us.'

'But what about Ukraine?' Jake asked. It was almost a snap, but he held it back. He wanted to understand and that was all I could ask.

I stared hard at the table and took a deep breath.

'Nothing I say should be taken as a justification for what has happened. There is no excuse, nor will there ever be, for war in the name of ego and the devastation of innocent lives.

When it comes to Ukraine, I am afraid my simple answer will leave you incredulous. But it is the best I can offer you. It was a demonstration of strength, to reinforce a dictator's grip on power. How could the Russian people tolerate such an action? As I said, Russia is a nation which has many borders and whose national conscience is fueled by fears of attack and betrayal. And one of the things the Russian people feared most was NATO.

NATO was a cold war military alliance formed in order to defend itself from the Soviet Union and the specter of communism. After the Berlin wall was brought down and Russia rejoined the world stage, we could not understand why NATO still existed. But not only did it go on existing, it expanded. It grew right across Europe, into former soviet states and further into the Baltic countries, right up to Russia's border. Russia made intimations that they should be invited to join. These were soundly rejected.

To Western eyes this all seemed reasonable. NATO did not intend to attack Russia, that notion was silly. It was strictly a defensive expansion of NATO's borders. But in Russia, polls showed that nearly two thirds of Russian people were fearful of this expansion and saw it as an immediate threat to peace and to Russia. Of course we did, we were being told daily by those who wanted absolute power that we should be fearful and that only they were the solution.

That does not mean that NATO were to blame for the war - that is a ridiculous notion born of propaganda - but NATO were the dragon that the Russian people were taught to fear. And every dictator needs a dragon to scare the populace with. Be it NATO, cultural destruction, religious piety, immigration etc. If we can understand that, perhaps we can guard against such propagation of fear in the future.

In The West there is a perception of immunity to this type of dictatorship. But the flares of warning were firing there too. With every small infraction to our governmental norms, glossed over by politicians and moved on from by a hungry media, we lose a shred of our democratic integrity. A parliament prorogued to avoid inconvenient votes. A law changed to save a political career mired in corruption. A man allowed to go on leading after breaking his own laws, for the sake of the political ambitions of those around him. The loser of a free and fair election, calling the result into question. A politician encouraging his supporters to rise up against the peaceful transfer of power. An election postponed for a spurious reason - a storm, an international crisis, the passing of a national icon. An election cancelled, as it had been postponed for such a long time anyway. No more elections needed, because it is the right thing for the country at this present time. There are dragons out there, but fear not, your government will slay them. We just need you to give us more power and for your children to pick up our weapons. A small price to pay for your safety.

War is not waged by normal people. It is waged by mad men with unquenchable egos, who push buttons behind desks while their countrymen die. But when nuclear war happens, no one is blameless. There must come a point when the people of the world see these men for what they are and stop giving them the reins of power.

Unquestioning loyalty to leadership is the source of all of humankind's wars and war crimes. Whether to politics or religion, we must be vigilant of and always question those who lead us. We must constantly remind them that they are accountable for their actions and they only lead us because we allow them too. There will always be more of us than them. A soldier *can* refuse to fight if he believes the cause to be nefarious. The people who surround dictators can *at any time*, band together and remove them in the name of peace. Men, women and everyone in between can take to the street the moment a leader beats a single note on the drums of aggression. We must realise that there is no war if we all collectively refuse to fight one. But of course, that is a difficult thing to do when we're all so scared of each other.

It seems to me that our technology has evolved faster than our ability to learn from and integrate with each other. We're more connected but more isolated and we haven't had the time to make that work yet. And humans, like every other animal on this planet, default to cautiousness and fear when faced with uncertainty. So we turn to cheap words and rhetoric, instead of trusting our better judgment and the good of our fellow man. This allows those who would take advantage of us to gain the power they crave, like rabid dogs chasing a thirst they can never quench.

We had the power to stop these mad men. Not just the Russian dictator, but the ones in the West who found the escalation of global conflict to be a convenient political distraction. There were so many wasted chances along the way to war. But we were all too scared to act. We *felt* powerless, so we gave up our power to the worst of mankind. And they used it to ruin us all.'

44

Quiet settled over the cool, dusty room. None of us made eye contact with each other, all lost in our own thoughts and grief, staring at the floor for answers.

'I'm sorry,' I said. It was all I could think of to say.

I scanned the room in search of my fate. I had tried to tell them the truth as I knew it, without fear or favor. None of it mattered now anyway, but with all that had happened I wouldn't have blamed them if they had sent me away, back to the cold of a small boat, desperate and alone.

After a moment, Karen looked up and placed her hand on my arm, A tear held firm in her eye.

'It's not your fault Carl. Erm, *Vasili.* Like you said, we're all to blame. We let it happen and we're all guilty. And there's nothing we can do about it now.'

Finally, Maisie turned from her intense focus on the kitchen window. She looked at me, her face still cold, but a touch of warmth seeping into her eyes.

'So what *do* we call you? I'm having trouble getting used to your… real name.'

I thought for a beat. It was not something I'd considered to this point, so used as I was, to responding to the name I'd offered them.

'Vasili lived a life in hiding, trained to be suspicious of everyone and never to trust a soul. On the surface he had a normal job and lived a normal life. But in reality it was one of fear, isolation and shadows. Carl lives a life a million miles away from that, on the very edge of existence. A much harder life, with much worse things to fear. But, he has friends.'

It was almost a question. I looked at Jake, who gave me the slightest of nods. It was all the encouragement I needed to continue.

'Carl's friends have given him a purpose, a reason to live, which is so much more than mere survival. If it's all the same to you, I think I would rather be Carl'

There was a noise outside the kitchen door, the sound of something being knocked over and whispers of blame. With a mother's instinct Karen ordered the kids into the kitchen. We'd been talking so long that they had woken up. Sensing the adults were not to be interrupted, they'd hunkered down to listen outside. They looked guilty and sullen as they entered the room, but Karen drew them close into a bear hug.

'How about Uncle Carl?' she asked, smiling at me. And the tears came then. I could not have been more grateful.

45

Many years have passed since I began this journal. My intention originally, was to keep a diary of my survival, to keep me sane while I scratched a living alone on the edge of the world. I thought that somehow if I died but society lived on, one day this journal may be found and I would be remembered by someone somewhere. In a strange way this thought would give me a reason to keep going, instead of hurling myself into the sea.

I never expected to be found by others, especially those I would befriend and survive with. The people who came to this island filled the gap that this journal was supposed to bandage over. They became my reason and my purpose to keep going. And so I stopped writing it. I had all but forgotten about it in fact, until this day. The 16th birthday of my first child. The first of three. Two girls, one boy.

The party goes on up at the big house and Maisie is doing a terrific job making it feel like one, with what little we have. I nipped back to the house to get the boy his present, something I brought with me on the day I came to the island. Searching for it at the back of the drawer where I'd hidden it, I found this diary and have been turning through the pages somewhat in awe.

It has brought back some deep and terrifying memories, but also a feeling of tremendous pride. For we have built a life for ourselves here, a tough one to be sure, but a life of more than survival without a doubt. A life that grows and continues to prosper despite our hardships.

But nevertheless, a story should have an ending and this journal of mine should be no different. So this then, will be the last entry. When it is done, I will take it and bury it in a tin at the top of the island.

If you have found it, for whatever reason, I hope you are well. I hope society has been able to rebuild from the small pockets of survival that exist in the isolated corners of the world that weathered the thousand years' storm.

If I can tell you one thing, let it be this: Learn from our lessons. Our way of living was lost because we let the politics of fear and division triumph over our better natures and trust in our fellow man. Do not make that same mistake. Call out those who would divide us, reach out to those you don't well understand or know. Be the person that takes on the risk of the first step to friendship.

Life is hard here on our little island, but we go on. We have found others like us, scattered over large distances but willing to form a loose community based on our common purpose of survival. We trade, sometimes with one side only able to provide a token gesture in return for what they need. And we do so with warm hearts. For if we are to survive and prosper, we know that one day we may be the ones in need. And it is the heart of the person we don't know, that will decide whether we get what we need or we perish.

So from our struggle here on this island to yours wherever you are, I wish you well. I hope your life is a good one, filled with the friendship and relationships I have come to know only in the second half of mine. I hope you have warmth, shelter and enough to eat, always. Fare you well, stranger.

Carl.

Author's Note

This is a work of fiction, which was begun in the dead of night, on a plane full of sleeping people, some 4 years ago now. Any resemblance to actual persons, living or dead, or actual events is purely coincidental yada yada, etc etc. You believe that, right?

Truth be told though, this story started off as just a hard-boiled survival thriller - I wanted to throw a guy into (and subsequently out of), a boat in the middle of the ocean in the black of night and just kind of see where it went. Somehow though, Carl surprised me (and yes Walking Dead fans, it was a hat tip) and ended up having far more depth than I'd intended. So the story went from a straight-up trashy thriller to something that wanted to be a bit more. It do be like that sometimes, with writing.

Of course, some of you may still think it's pretty trashy. Some of you may think it's just straight up trash (heck, I might be one of you). But whatever you think, I want to thank you for reading it. A great deal of work goes into writing something of this length; endless hours spent staring at a screen hammering keys in a trance, not to mention the sleepless nights or banging of one's head against hard surfaces when the story isn't quite coming out right.

At its best, writing a novel is a high unlike any other - and this is why in spite of our increasingly digital world, people still do it. When there's no distractions, the story feels right and the words are flying, you feel like someone has wired you into the mainframe of the universe. You're not a writer anymore, just a pen which something far more powerful is using to tell a story that *must* be told. There's nothing like that feeling.

At its worst though, you feel like the story is there, but you're not telling it right. Or the words won't come and you only have 20 minutes left before you have to get back to the real world. Or you're acutely, *painfully* aware that you've spent several months of your life writing the world's worst story, which no one will ever. want. to. read.

Why am I telling you this? Because the words 'thank you' just don't do enough to convey how grateful I feel towards anyone who would take the time to read my scribblings. The pain of all those long sessions spent feeling like I'm a terrible writer and I'm wasting my time is zapped away in a heartbeat, when someone says they read what I wrote. Even if they hated it, it doesn't matter. Somebody read my story. It was worth writing. Thank God. And thank *you* again, for taking the time to read it and giving me that validation.

The further I got with this story the more aware I was of how tough a sell it was going to be. Like who wants to read about a low-level spy escaping a nuclear war? How 1980's is that? The world's moved on dude! But I finished it, because from time to time the damned thing would just pound everything else out of my head and demand to be written. After I finished it, I sent it around the literary agent circuit without gaining a great deal of interest and eventually shelved it. I was disappointed, but quite pragmatic about it: It was fun to write and exercised some demons, now time to write that other thing that you keep telling yourself you're not ready to write. And that was that.

And then about a year later, February 2022 happened. And suddenly the story didn't seem so stupid anymore. Suddenly I was wondering what *I* would do if the missiles came. This story was intended as a warning and a plea for understanding and diplomacy on both sides. Though it feels somewhat pointless now, given the stark madness of this Russian dictator, I still believe the central message has value: We must be smarter about who we allow to lead us and more understanding of people and cultures we don't know much about. Though it eases our fears to hear tough talk, we must not continue allowing those who preach aggression and intolerance to hold the keys to power. There will always be more of us than there are of them. A better world starts with us.

And to those of you who surround such a leader, the ones who do their bidding without question in the name of your own political ambition: **you are the most to blame**. It will not be the crazy man who eventually destroys the world, it will be the sane ones who stood close by and let him do it.

Thank you again for reading. I wish you all the best.

Chris Wilde, February 2022.

Also by Christopher Wilde:

Kissing the Plate

Just Another Young Player

***

chriswildewriting@outlook.com

@CWildeWriting

www.chriswildewriting.com

Printed in Great Britain
by Amazon

21374507R00192